NANCY

FRIENDS OR ENEMIES?

I paused, feeling helpless as I peered ahead into the shadowy reaches of the rigging. Where had the guy gone? Had he pulled too far ahead for me to catch him? Or had he, perhaps, doubled back and come around behind me, waiting for the chance to sneak up and make another attempt to push me to my doom?

At that moment the emcee paused briefly in his patter. In the brief seconds of relative quiet, I heard a sort of grunting sound just off to my right. Aha!

Moving as silently as I could, I headed in that direction. There was an enormous light fixture in my way. I carefully maneuvered myself over it to the other side—and froze.

Two teenage boys were crouched on a beam just a few feet away, staring back at me.

NANCY DREW
girl detective®

#1 Without a Trace
#2 A Race Against Time
#3 False Notes
#4 High Risk
#5 Lights, Camera . . .
#6 Action!
#7 The Stolen Relic
#8 The Scarlet Macaw Scandal
#9 Secret of the Spa
#10 Uncivil Acts
#11 Riverboat Ruse
#12 Stop the Clock
#13 Trade Wind Danger
#14 Bad Times, Big Crimes
#15 Framed
#16 Dangerous Plays
#17 En Garde
#18 Pit of Vipers
#19 Orchid Thief
#20 Getting Burned
#21 Close Encounters
#22 Dressed to Steal
#23 Troubled Waters
#24 Murder on the Set

THE HARDY BOYS
UNDERCOVER BROTHERS®

#1 Extreme Danger
#2 Running on Fumes
#3 Boardwalk Bust
#4 Thrill Ride
#5 Rocky Road
#6 Burned
#7 Operation: Survival
#8 Top Ten Ways to Die
#9 Martial Law
#10 Blown Away
#11 Hurricane Joe
#12 Trouble in Paradise
#13 The Mummy's Curse
#14 Hazed
#15 Death and Diamonds

GIRL DETECTIVE®

NANCY DREW

AND THE

UNDERCOVER BROTHERS®

HARDY BOYS

Super Mystery

TERROR ON TOUR

CAROLYN KEENE

and

FRANKLIN W. DIXON

Aladdin Paperbacks

NEW YORK LONDON TORONTO SYDNEY

ALADDIN PAPERBACKS
An imprint of Simon & Schuster Children's Publishing Division
1230 Avenue of the Americas, New York, NY 10020

Designed by Karin Paprocki
The text of this book was set in Meridien.
Manufactured in the United States of America
First Aladdin Paperbacks edition June 2007
10
Library of Congress Control Number 2006935186
ISBN-13: 978-1-4169-2726-6
ISBN-10: 1-4169-2726-3
0912 OFF

CONTENTS

TERROR ON TOUR

CHAPTER 1

JOE

SPECIAL DELIVERY

I stared into the muzzle of the gun.

"What now?" I whispered.

My brother, Frank, shot me a dirty look. That wasn't easy, since we were tied together by our arms, which were twisted behind our backs. It was like something from a James Bond movie. Except we didn't have any of those cool devices Bond always uses to free himself.

"I told you we should've been more careful," Frank hissed at me. "But *no*—why scope out the place from the outside first when you can run right in like a doofus?"

Maybe he was right. It *was* sort of my idea to sneak in through that open window . . . which just happened to land us right in front of Thug #1 and Thug #2. The pair was part of a gang that had been trying to sell drugs to elementary school kids all over the county. Which probably tells you they weren't exactly upstanding citizens.

But it was way too late for should-haves. We were here now, staring down the muzzle of an ugly-looking pistol in an abandoned house in the worst section of Bayport. I guessed the room we were in had once been the dining room. There was a big wooden table shoved up against one wall and a chandelier hanging right over our heads. There was only one window, and it was covered by a dusty brown curtain. That meant nobody was going to wander by and see us being held at gunpoint.

We were on our own.

I looked at our captors. There were two of them—a short, skinny bald dude and a tall, fat guy with breath so bad I could smell it from where I was sitting at least five feet away. The bald guy was the one with the gun.

"So *you're* the famous Hardy brothers," the fat guy said. "You two don't seem so tough to me."

He let out a snort. I think it was supposed to be a laugh.

"Let us go," Frank spoke up. "You know you'll never get away with this. You might as well release us right now before someone gets hurt. If you turn yourselves in, the police will go easy on you."

Yeah, like that's going to work! I thought as both dudes busted out laughing. After about a million of these ATAC missions, you'd think Frank would figure out that the bad guys hardly ever respond to earnest calls for doing the right thing.

Still, his little speech had served one purpose. The bad guys couldn't stop cracking up. Maybe we could use that to our advantage?

"On three," I whispered to Frank.

"What?" Frank sounded confused.

The bald guy stopped laughing and glared at me. "What did you say, Yellow?"

I gritted my teeth. For some reason, the goons had decided to address Frank as "Hardy" while I got to be "Yellow." I assumed it was because of my blond hair, but still. Not the coolest nickname ever, you know?

"My name's Joe," I said. "J-O-E. Even a dimwit like you should be able to pronounce that."

"Keep on joking, Yellow," the fat man growled. He leaned a little closer, giving me another whiff of his breath. It reminded me of our pet parrot, Playback. His cage smells kind of like that when it hasn't been cleaned for a while. "We'll see how funny you are when Farley gets here."

Oh, right. Farley. I had no idea who this Farley guy was, or what he was planning to do to us. But I really didn't want to find out.

It was time for action.

"One, two, three!" I yelled.

I sprang to my feet and leaped at the goons.

That's what I meant to do, anyway. Unfortunately, Frank hadn't exactly caught on to my plan. He just sat there, which meant I found myself leaping forward about half an inch, then landing back on my butt with a loud *oof.*

Bad Breath cracked up. "Smooth move, Yellow," he said with a chortle.

The bald guy didn't look so amused. "That was *not* a smart idea," he snapped. He took a step closer and raised his gun a little. "Not smart at all."

"Nice backup plan, Joe," Frank said. "Bet you spent, like, *hours* thinking that one up."

I hate it when he gets sarcastic. It's *so* not amusing.

"Maybe we shouldn't wait for Farley," Baldy said, his eyes glittering. "Maybe we should just—"

Ding dong!

The fat guy blinked. "Hey," he said. "Was that the doorbell? Maybe it's Farley."

The other guy rolled his eyes. "Yeah," he said. "I'm so sure he'd just walk up and ring the doorbell."

Sarcasm came a lot more naturally to him than it did to Frank.

"Keep an eye on them," Baldy added. "I'll go get rid of whoever it is."

If I craned my neck way to the left, I could just see the door from where we were sitting. I watched Baldy walk into the front room and peer through the little window next to the door.

"What the . . . ," he muttered.

"Who is it?" Frank wriggled behind me. "What's happening?"

"Quit it! You're cutting off my circulation."

"Shut up," Bad Breath told us. Then he took a few steps toward the door. "Who's out there?"

"Pizza guy," Baldy called back.

Pizza guy? I thought, with a sudden flash of hope.

The fat guy looked confused. "Did we order a pizza?"

"Of course not!" the other guy snapped. "He obviously has the wrong house. I'll get rid of him." He put his hand on the doorknob, then paused and glanced back at Frank and me. "Then again, maybe another hostage isn't such a bad idea, considering . . ."

Uh-oh! I leaned even farther to the side to see better. Baldy tucked his gun in the back waistband of his pants, then opened the door. A slim, dark-skinned young man was standing there with a big white pizza box held out in front of him.

"Pizza delivery," he said. His voice sounded familiar. In fact, he sounded a lot like one of our associates.

"Pizza, huh?" Baldy said. His voice sounded much more pleasant than it had a second ago. It was like he'd morphed from a drug-dealing thug into a kindly middle-aged college professor. "Oh, dear. We didn't order any pizza. But why don't you come inside while we get this sorted out?"

Watch it! I thought.

"Of course, sir," the pizza guy said to Baldy. "Thank you very much."

A second later he was standing in the front room with the door shut behind him. That's when Baldy pulled out his pistol.

"Okay, pizza boy," he growled. "Put your hands where I can see them."

"All right, sir." The pizza guy sounded calm. "But what would you like me to do with the pizza?"

"What?" Baldy sounded confused. "Hey!" he added. Now he sounded surprised—and maybe scared?

"What's happening?" Frank hissed, wriggling again. "Joe, is that who I think it—"

"Shh!" I hushed him.

The fat guy took another step toward the door. "Hey, what's going on?"

The pizza guy was smiling now. "You might want to drop that gun, sir. Please."

He tossed aside the pizza box. Now, everyone except poor Frank could see the long, deadly-looking rifle the man was holding, which currently was jabbed into Baldy's gut.

The fat guy lurched forward. "Freeze," the pizza guy said, still smiling pleasantly. "Or things will have to get ugly."

Bad Breath froze. Baldy muttered a few choice words under his breath, but then he slowly leaned down and set his pistol on the floor. Then he straightened up and raised his hands.

"Thank you so much." The pizza guy took a few steps forward, jabbing Baldy along with the end of his rifle. "Frank, Joe—you two okay?"

I smiled weakly. "Yeah," I answered. "Thanks, Vijay."

A few minutes later it was all over. I stood there rubbing my rope-burned wrists and watching a big, burly police officer snap a set of handcuffs on Baldy. Bad Breath had already been dragged off to the waiting squad car.

"Whoa," I commented to Frank beside me. "That was sort of an embarrassing end to the mission."

Frank shrugged. "The important thing is those two jerks are going to jail. With a little luck, they'll rat out the rest of the gang."

"Yeah," I muttered. "Too bad Vijay will get all the credit for it. I can see the headlines now: 'Local Pizza Dude Nabs Drug Lords.'"

It was sort of humiliating. Still, if someone had to step in and save us, I was glad it was Vijay Patel. Vijay is one cool dude. He's a member of the local ATAC—American Teens Against Crime. Frank and I have known him for ages. That's because our father started the organization, and the two of us were ATAC's very first recruits.

Dad's a private investigator and former New York City cop. His lifelong dream was to form a national organization of teenagers that would help law enforcement fight crime in all the places where an adult cop or FBI agent would stick out like a sore thumb. Once he retired from the force, he went ahead and formed ATAC.

Everybody in Bayport knows that Frank and I are amateur detectives. We solve local crimes here and there, and we've had our photos in the newspaper more than once. But nobody except Dad and the others in ATAC knows the whole truth. Not our best friends, not our teachers, not even our mother or our aunt Trudy, who lives with us.

I turned to watch the cops drag Baldy out of the house. Frank was watching too.

"Come on," he said. "Guess we should get out of here."

When we got outside, I saw Vijay standing in the weedy front yard. He spotted us and walked over.

"You guys okay?" he asked.

"Yeah," Frank said. "Thanks for coming to the rescue. How'd you know we were in trouble?"

Vijay shrugged. "I didn't." He looked around, obviously checking to make sure nobody else was close enough to overhear what he was saying. "I was tailing you, waiting for a good chance to hand over your next mission. When I saw you sneak into that house and not come out for a while, I figured I'd better check it out."

"Another mission?" I said, my mood suddenly soaring upward. "Hand it over!" I was more than ready to get back on top of my game.

ATAC mission CDs look like ordinary music or video game disks, and after one viewing, that's exactly what they become. But on their first play, they give us all the details of our next assignment. Vijay was sometimes the one to deliver a new mission CD, usually inside a pizza box.

Vijay pulled something out of his pocket. It looked like a coupon book for the local pizza place. But it was more than large enough to have a CD tucked inside.

I grabbed for it, but Frank got it first. "Thanks, V," he said, sticking it into his pocket. "For everything."

"Rock on, guys," Vijay said. With a salute, he took off back toward the center of town.

"Sweet!" I commented as Frank and I headed down the block toward where we'd left our motorcycles. "Can't wait to see what's next." I grimaced as the cop car pulled out from the curb and sped past us. "Let's hope this time we actually manage to handle the mission all on our own."

CHAPTER 

NANCY

EXCITING NEWS

"Nancy! Hey, Nancy Drew! Over here!"

I looked up at the sound of my name. My boyfriend, Ned Nickerson, was waving at me from an empty table halfway across the crowded mall food court.

"There he is," I told my friends Bess Marvin and George Fayne. They had just stepped away from the counter of one of the fast-food places nearby.

George glanced toward Ned, her mouth still stuck in the scowl she'd been wearing for the past half hour. "Why did I let you people talk me into coming to the mall?" she muttered. "And on a weekend, no less."

"Because I promised to buy you lunch if you'd help me pick out a new bathing suit." Bess shifted her food tray from one hand to the other as she grabbed a handful of napkins from the dispenser on the counter. "Now come on, let's get over there before someone pushes Ned down and steals his table."

I laughed as George rolled her eyes. George and Bess are cousins, although you'd never guess it by looking at them. George is the ultimate tomboy—short hair, jeans and sneakers, minimal makeup. Bess, on the other hand, adores pretty clothes and always looks perfect from the top of her blond head to the toes of her designer shoes. She'll happily spend hours at the mall trying on the latest fashions.

As for me, I tend to hover somewhere in the middle. My fashion style is classic yet comfortable, and I try to remember to run a brush through my strawberry-blond hair before leaving the house. I like shopping just fine—unless there's something more interesting to do, like working on a case.

Oh yeah. Did I mention I like solving mysteries?

But the only mystery happening at the mall that Sunday afternoon was how much more crowded it could get before we were violating the fire codes. It was a sweltering midsummer day outside, and it seemed everyone in River Heights had decided to take advantage of the free air-conditioning.

"Good thing we arranged to meet Ned here during his lunch break," I commented as we wended our way between tables. "Otherwise we'd never find a place to sit."

"Yeah, and then we'd have to leave," George said. "Big bummer."

Bess and I ignored her. George likes to complain about clothes shopping, but she *loves* checking out the newest computer equipment and electronic gadgets at Wired World, her favorite store at the mall, and we'd already spent half an hour there before beginning the search for the perfect swimsuit. Luckily Bess likes that store, too—she's surprisingly handy, and is just as likely to spend a Saturday afternoon tinkering under the hood of her car or rewiring her parents' basement as she is to spend it getting her nails done or shopping for clothes. As for me, I'd managed to keep myself occupied by listening to music on one of the store's sample MP3 players.

Finally we reached Ned's table. I set down my tray, which held a tuna salad sandwich and a soda. "Sorry we're a little late," I told Ned. "Bess just had to try on one last bikini before we came to meet you."

"Actually, it was *three,*" George interjected, flopping down into a chair and unwrapping her burrito. "But who's counting?"

"Good thing you got here when you did," Ned said, a mischievous twinkle in his eyes. "I was just about to give up on you and give away these extra tickets I got at work."

"What tickets?" I asked, only half tuned in to what

he was saying as I poked my straw through the lid of my soda. Ned works part-time during the school year and full-time during the summer at the office of the *River Heights Bugle*, the newspaper his father publishes. He's always getting free stuff through work: movie passes, gift baskets, coupons for free car washes, stuff like that.

Ned pulled a few tickets out of his pocket. Bess leaned closer to see them.

"No way!" she shrieked so loudly that people at the tables around us shot us startled glances. "You got Rockapazooma tickets?"

That got my attention right away. "Are you serious?" I exclaimed. "That concert's been sold out for months!"

Rockapazooma was the biggest thing to hit the river cities region in years. More than a dozen bands were scheduled to play on a big patch of farmland halfway between River Heights and Farmingville. Among them were some of the biggest names in popular music, like hip-hop superstar DJ Razz, award-winning singer-songwriter Toni Lovely, and the hot new pop band the Royal We.

Ned grinned. "Not for someone with the right connections," he said. "The *Bugle* wants me to cover the show for them—you know, get the teen perspective. And of course I mentioned that it wouldn't be the real experience if I had to go alone. . . ."

"I call one of the tickets!" George yelped, grabbing for the tickets in his hand.

Ned pulled them out of reach just in time. "Relax, there are enough for all four of us."

"Wow, Rockapazooma!" I glanced at my friends. "Weren't we just wondering what we were going to do for fun next weekend?"

"Not anymore!" George grinned. "The show is going to be awesome—I can't believe I'm actually going to see Lethal Injection live!"

"Lethal Injection?" Bess rolled her eyes. "Out of all the great bands that are going to be there, *that's* the one you're excited about? Grown men prancing around in monster makeup, screaming at the top of their lungs?"

Lethal Injection is a heavy metal band whose members never appear in public without their trademark neon makeup, long hair, and wild leather costumes. I wasn't too familiar with their music, but based on their gimmicky look and name, I figured I probably wasn't missing much.

George shrugged. "You should give them a chance," she said. "My little brother has both their albums, and they totally rock."

"Hmm." Bess didn't look convinced. "Well, I can't wait to see Toni Lovely. She's one of my favorites."

"I still think you only like her 'cause she looks like you," I teased. I'd noticed the likeness the first time I'd seen one of the performer's videos on TV. Toni Lovely is a little skinnier, and she doesn't have Bess's dimples. But both of them have the same blond hair, sweet smile, and peaches-and-cream complexion. Nobody would ever mistake them for identical twins, but there's definitely a strong resemblance.

Ned gave Bess a careful look. "Hey, I never really thought about it before, but she *does* look sort of like you. Like she could be your older sister or something."

"Maybe she's my true long-lost cousin, and she and George were switched at birth," Bess joked.

George let out a snort. "That would explain a lot, actually."

"Well, I love her music too, even though she looks nothing like me," I said. "I also think it's cool that she produced that TV special about the rain forest."

"Yeah, definitely." Ned nodded and took a sip of his soda. "Actually, all the bands on the bill are known for their support of the environment. That's the whole point of this concert, remember?"

In all the excitement of finding out about the tickets, I'd almost forgotten. "Oh yeah," I said. "I've heard all the profits are going to environmental causes. The music acts all volunteered to donate their time. Very cool."

Bess looked skeptical. "Even Lethal Injection?" she asked. "They don't exactly seem like the do-gooder types."

"You'd be surprised," Ned told her. "I know I was when I started doing some research this morning for my story. It turns out those guys have raised more money for environmental causes than any other band on the bill—even more than the Royal We, and everyone knows they're all about the environment."

I nodded. "I just saw the lead singer of the Royal We doing a TV interview. She was talking about deforestation in Africa or something like that."

"That's Kijani," Ned said. "She's originally from some little country in Africa. She's really passionate about her causes, and very well-spoken considering she's only twenty years old."

"Yeah, I love her accent," Bess said. Then she seemed to be hit with a sudden thought. "Wait a second—I think I just saw something about her in one of those tabloids at the grocery store. Isn't she dating one of the members of Lethal Injection?"

I raised one eyebrow at her. "The tabloids?"

Bess blushed. "It was on the cover," she said. "It's not like I was actually *reading* it. Anyway, they showed the guy without his makeup, and he's actually kind of cute."

"Interesting. I guess that's cool," George said, grinning. "But he'd better have his makeup back on in time for the concert. I can't wait to see who gets killed on stage. Since it's Rockapazooma, maybe they'll *all* commit suicide!"

"What are you talking about?" I asked, confused.

George stared at me. "Do you live on this planet, Nancy?" she said. "That's LI's whole shtick! At every one of their live shows there's a murder or suicide."

"Staged, of course," Ned put in.

"Duh." George reached across the table to steal one of Ned's French fries. "I hear half the fun of their shows is trying to figure out who's going to get offed that night and how."

I wasn't sure that sounded like much fun at all—I have too many real criminals coming in and out of my life to want to look for that sort of thing in my entertainment—but I decided to withhold judgment until I saw their performance for myself. In the meantime I was already looking forward to seeing some of my favorite artists perform live.

"Ned, did I ever mention that you're the greatest?" I shivered with anticipation. "This concert is going to be epic!"

We were still discussing Rockapazooma as we wandered down the mall aisle half an hour later. Bess interrupted herself in the middle of gushing over Toni Lovely's latest single to point to a swimsuit in the window we were passing.

"Ooo, check it out!" she exclaimed. "That's exactly the color I was looking for at the other store. Do you mind if I just run in and—"

"Ned Nickerson!" a new voice interrupted her. "Fancy seeing you here."

I swallowed a groan of dismay. Only one person I knew had a voice that supercilious, smug, and self-satisfied: Deirdre Shannon.

My friends and I have known Deirdre since she moved to town the summer after third grade, and Deirdre has been crushing on Ned for almost that long. Even though he's never shown the slightest romantic interest in her, she refuses to give up hope. And no wonder—Ned might be the only thing Deirdre has ever wanted that she couldn't get. You know that old saying "You can't buy happiness"? Well, Deirdre seems to be on a one-person quest to prove it wrong. "Hi, Deirdre," I said, trying to hide my lack of enthusiasm.

Deirdre didn't bother responding to my greeting. Completely ignoring me, Bess, and George, she worked her many shopping bags into one hand and sidled up to Ned with a coy smile. "Shouldn't you be at work, young man?" she asked. "Who's covering all that breaking news while you're not at your desk?"

"Right," George muttered. "Because there's usually all kinds of breaking news here in River Heights—riots, erupting volcanoes, Martians landing in Bluff View Park . . ."

George isn't a fan of Deirdre's. None of us are, really, but George seems to take Deirdre's many annoying qualities much more personally than Bess or I do.

Meanwhile Ned merely chuckled politely. He's not a Deirdre fan either, but he hides it better than the rest of us. He's way too nice to come right out and tell her she has a better chance of going out with one of those Martians in Bluff View Park than she does with him.

"I'm on my lunch break," he told Deirdre. "Figured I'd come over here for some of River Ron's world-famous fries."

"You should have texted me," Deirdre cooed. "Daddy represented River Ron's once in court—I can get all the food I want there for free."

"Oops, did Ned forget to text you again, DeeDee?" George said. "I guess he also forgot to save you a ticket for Rockapazooma. Too bad; we'll have to buy you a T-shirt."

"So you guys are going to Rockapazooma? Whoop-di-doo," Deirdre retorted. "I've had my ticket for weeks. It's a premium ticket, of course, which means I'll have access to the whole backstage area." She smirked. "Did I mention that several of the performers are friends of mine? Like Kijani from the Royal We, and Nick Needles from Lethal Injection . . ."

"Really?" Bess said, sounding interested.

"No way." George frowned. "You don't know those guys."

Deirdre shrugged, shifting her shopping bags to her other hand. "I don't care if you believe me or not. It's true." She tilted her head up to smile at Ned. "Maybe we can meet up at the show, and I can introduce you around."

"Maybe." Ned checked his watch. "Oops, look at the time! I've got to get back to work—breaking news waits for no one, you know. Enjoy your shopping, Deirdre."

"Thanks." Deirdre looked disappointed. "I'll see you around, Ned."

"Not if he sees you first," George said as all four of us hurried away.

Bess shot one last wistful glance at the store window as we rounded the corner toward the mall's exit. "Guess I can finish my bathing suit search another day," she said. "It's not like we'll be hanging out at the pool next weekend anyway. We'll be too busy going to Rockapazooma!"

I grinned. "I still can't believe we're going."

"I can't believe Deirdre will be there too," George complained. "If we run into her, she'll probably ruin the whole experience by following us around and bragging about knowing celebrities and stuff."

"Oh, come on," Ned told her. "They're expecting two hundred thousand people at the show. With that kind of crowd, what are the odds of running into one particular person?"

CHAPTER 3

FRANK

A NEW MISSION

"Pop it in, already!" Joe said.

I glanced at him. He was jumping around like an overcaffeinated monkey. Then again, that could pretty well describe my brother most of the time. He isn't what you'd call patient.

"I'm working on it," I told him.

I couldn't resist slowing my movements a little just to bug him. First I slid the CD slooowly out from between the pages of the ad booklet. I took my time as I made a leisurely stroll across my bedroom toward the game console on my desk. My hand moved like molasses as I reached toward the power button. . . .

"Frank!" Joe exclaimed.

I grinned. Joe is way too easy to mess with sometimes.

But I didn't make him suffer any longer. I was just as eager as he was to see what our next mission would be. I slid the CD into the machine and hit Play.

"Greetings, ATAC agents," said the familiar voice of Q., our boss at ATAC. *"Your next mission begins in six days, and involves out-of-state travel. Please press Continue if you would like to accept the mission. Your briefing will follow."*

"No brainer." Joe lunged for the console and pressed the button.

I opened my mouth to remind him that we're supposed to be a team, and that it would be nice if he consulted me before pressing Continue. Or before climbing through a window in an abandoned house, for that matter.

But then I shut it again. Joe will never change. Besides, the message was starting.

A silvery flash filled the screen, and the ear-shattering scream of an electric guitar poured out of the speakers. I cast a nervous glance at the bedroom door, hoping Mom and Aunt Trudy were still safely downstairs.

When I looked at the screen again, it was filled with smoke. A dark figure strode out from the middle of it, carrying a microphone. He had shaggy dark hair and was wearing leather pants and a mask.

"Hello ATAC agents!" the mystery man on the screen shrieked into the microphone. *"Are you ready to rock? Because you're going to Rockapazooma!"*

"Whoa!" Joe exclaimed as the masked guy paused to

play a sizzling lick on his guitar. "Did you hear that? Rockapazooma!"

"Isn't that some big concert out in the Midwest?" I said. "I saw something about it on TV the other day."

Joe looked shocked. "It's not just *some* concert, dude," he said. "It's *the* concert!"

I shrugged. I like music as much as the next guy, but I'm not obsessed with it like Joe. He wears his DJ Razz T-shirt all the time. Aunt Trudy has forbidden him from wearing his Lethal Injection shirt, though. For some reason she thinks the picture of one band member holding up another band member's severed head is disgusting.

Onscreen, the guitar-playing guy was fading out. He was replaced by the image of crowds of people partying at an outdoor concert.

Q.'s voice continued the message in voice-over. *"Rockapazooma is more than just the biggest concert of the year. It's a way for musicians and sponsors to raise awareness of the environmental problems facing the world today: deforestation, endangered species, global warming, and other issues. All proceeds of the show will go to groups working to fight these problems. So not only will fans get to enjoy an entire day of great live music, but they'll be helping to save the world, too. Sounds like a win-win, right?"*

"Totally," Joe interjected with a grin. "Especially for us!"

"However," the voice continued, *"ATAC and its affiliated agencies have intercepted buzz indicating that someone may intend to disrupt the concert. Unfortunately we can't tell you much more than that. The stakes are high, and if the wrong people were to intercept this message, it could endanger the mission—and your lives."*

"Helpful," I commented.

Joe was grinning. "I can't believe we're really going to Rockapazooma!"

Way to stay on task, I thought. But I didn't say anything, because the voice-over was continuing.

"Your identities for this mission are Jack and Jimmy Leyland, ordinary music fans. You will have to stay on the lookout for anything suspicious. We may try to mobilize another set of agents to work on this case as well, but you should proceed as if you are the only agents present. We are working closely with the local police department and FBI office on this case, so if you run into any serious trouble, please consider them your allies. A crowd-control tool is included in the CD case in case you run into any trouble. As usual this mission is top secret. Good luck, and rock on, ATACers. This CD will be reformatted in five seconds. Five, four, three, two, one . . ."

I steeled myself for more screaming guitars when the disk switched to music. Instead, a female voice poured out of the speakers. The song was catchy, but I didn't recognize it.

"Who's this?" I asked.

Joe stared at me. "Man, you're even more out of touch than I thought. It's only the Royal We, the hottest new band in the known world."

"The Royal We?" It rang a bell. "Wait, isn't that the band with the young female singer—"

"Who's amazingly hot?" Joe finished for me. "Yeah, her name's Kijani."

"I was going to say, the young female singer who sought asylum here from her home country in Africa." I searched my mind for the details. I'd read a story on the singer a few weeks ago in a news magazine. "She's part of a royal family, I think. That's how they came up with the idea for the name of the band."

"Whatever." Joe shrugged.

"Joe, we're not going to Rockapazooma to look at girls," I reminded him.

Joe grinned. "The guy on the CD said to watch out for anything suspicious," he said. "I'll be keeping my eye out for suspiciously hot girls."

I suddenly remembered something. "Hey, didn't the CD say something was included with it?" I grabbed for the jewel case, which I'd dropped on the desk near the game console.

Joe looked over my shoulder as I examined it. "What is it?" he asked. "Must be pretty small."

"Here we go." I spotted two cylindrical silvery objects tucked into the casing. Each was about the size and shape of a pack of breath mints. Joe grabbed one and I picked up the other.

I turned it over in my hands. The only thing breaking the smooth silver surface was a tiny button at one end. "I wonder how they—"

"YOW!" Joe yelled, jumping about three feet in the air. He dropped his tool and shook his right hand violently, hopping up and down and grimacing. "That thing has a serious *bite* to it! Take my advice, Frank—don't touch the end and press the button at the same time."

That's my brother—the human guinea pig. "So they're like miniature cattle prods." I figured that could definitely come in handy in a crowd full of rowdy concert-goers.

"Boys?" Aunt Trudy's voice floated through the door. "Is everything okay in there? What's with all the yelling?"

"We're fine, Aunt Trudy," I called back. "Sorry about the noise."

As her footsteps faded away, I looked at Joe. "That reminds me. How're we going to explain this one?"

Keeping our ATAC work a secret from Mom and Aunt Trudy is always a challenge. Dad helps us cover when he can. But mostly Joe and I just need to be really good at coming up with stories to explain our comings and goings.

"Easy," Joe said. "We tell the truth—sort of."

I blinked. "Huh?"

Joe grinned. "We say we're going to Rockapazooma,"

he said. "Lethal Injection and DJ Razz are both playing the show. Everybody knows I'm into them. So we say I called in to a radio contest or something, and won an all-expenses-paid trip for two to the show."

I had to admit it was a great plan. "Keep it simple," I said, echoing one of Dad's favorite sayings. "Yeah, that could work." Then I realized what he'd said and grimaced. "Lethal Injection, huh?"

"Yeah! I can't wait to see them live," Joe exclaimed. "It's going to be awesome! I wonder what the death stunt will be? Oh! And I hope they play 'White Hot Death'—that song rocks."

I couldn't help grinning at his enthusiasm, even if I didn't share it. "Yeah," I said. "Remind me to pack my earplugs, okay?"

"Whoa!" Joe climbed out of the taxi. "Check it out. This place is packed already."

I finished paying the driver. Then I straightened up and looked around.

Joe was right. The concert venue was a seething mass of humanity. Now that we were there, there was no question about why we might need those crowd-control devices if we were to do any investigating. We weren't even inside and we could barely move.

We were standing near the parking area, which was bumper to grill with vehicles. A tall chain-link fence blocked off the enormous field where the concert would take place. Through it I could see a huge stage surrounded by an equally huge spiderweb of lights and rigging. Sixty-foot-tall speaker towers stood on either side of the stage. Giant video screens atop more speakers dotted the football-field-size area in front of it.

I could also see people. Lots of people.

"And here I thought we were arriving nice and early," I said. "The music doesn't even start for more than an hour!"

"Well, we're here now." Joe headed toward the nearest entry point. "Let's get inside."

We waited in line for our turn. A bored-looking security guard glanced at our passes, which we'd picked up from the pilot of the private plane that had flown us in from Bayport that morning.

"Welcome to Rockapazooma." The guard stifled a yawn. He was wearing a neon green T-shirt with the concert's logo—a smiling planet Earth playing an electric guitar. It was kind of dorky, but it got the point across. "Are you carrying any liquids, weapons, or electronic devices?"

"No way," Joe answered for both of us. We took out our cell phones and pocket change and put them in the guy's little tray.

"Step through the metal detector and enjoy the show."

I thought about the mini-electric-prod in my jeans pocket. What if the metal detector picked it up and we got kicked out?

But I should have known ATAC would be on top of things. We both made it through the metal detector without a buzz.

"Guess those little shocker doodads don't have much metal in them," Joe commented as we stepped away.

"Yeah." I stuck my cell back in my pocket and glanced around. From inside the gates the place looked even more crowded. "I guess we should still follow our original plan—walk around and try to get a feel for the place before it gets any busier."

"Are you sure?" Joe teased. "You mean, you don't have a backup plan?"

I didn't bother to answer. I was still feeling kind of uneasy about the whole situation. It was weird not knowing what this mission was about. There had been times when ATAC had been more vague with us than I would have liked, but this took the cake.

Still, that didn't mean we couldn't attack it logically. Right?

"Let's make a circuit of the whole place," I suggested. "We can scope out the best places to see the crowd."

"The crowd?" Joe glanced toward the stage. A bunch

of roadies were up there moving equipment around. "What about the bands?"

I started walking. "We're not here to watch the bands."

"We're supposed to keep an eye on *everything,*" Joe pointed out. "That means the bands too."

"Whatever." I stopped and shaded my eyes against the sun. "Let's head for that speaker tower out in the middle first, and then—"

"Hey!" Joe grabbed my arm. "Check out the babe."

A young woman of about nineteen was doing some kind of solo interpretive dance nearby. Her eyes were closed, and her arms were waving over her head. She was dressed in nothing but a grass skirt and a skimpy bikini top that left very little to the imagination.

"We're not here for *that,* either," I told Joe. "Come on."

Joe shot one last glance at the teen. Then he jogged to catch up with me.

"You're not going to let me have any fun at all on this trip, are you?"

He was giving me the Look. I hate the Look. It makes me feel like I'm a hundred and one years older than Joe, instead of just one. It almost made me ashamed that I really *had* packed earplugs for this trip. They were in my jeans pocket right now, right next to the mini-cattle-prod. Good thing Joe didn't know that. Otherwise I'd probably be facing the Look times ten.

But I couldn't let it get to me. We had business to take care of. "Grow up, Joe," I told him. "We're here on a case, remember?"

"Yeah, I know," he said. "But that doesn't mean we can't have fun, too."

We were still moving through the crowd as we talked. At that moment we were off to the right side of the stage. Just ahead I noticed several security guards wearing those neon green planet shirts. They were standing in front of another chain-link fence. Behind it were a bunch of big gleaming charter-type buses and double-wide trailers.

Joe spotted them too. "That looks like the backstage area," he said. "Let's sneak in and take a look."

"Sneak in?" I glanced at the guards. Each of them alone easily weighed more than Joe and I did together. "I don't think so."

"Why not?" Joe said. "You're the one who's always saying we should be thorough, and—whoa! Check *her* out!"

Glancing where he was staring, I saw three girls about our own age. Unlike Ms. Bikini Dancer, they were all fully clothed in shorts and T-shirts. The slim girl with reddish-blond hair and the athletic-looking brunette were both cute. But their friend really stood out in the crowd. She was blond and curvy, with the kind of face that made you want to walk right up to her and say hi.

I realized I was staring. I also realized that Joe was already hurrying toward the girls.

Uh-oh. I took off after him.

"Hi," he was saying to the blond when I caught up. "I'm Joe. What's your—"

"Excuse us," I interrupted.

I grabbed his arm. He struggled a little, but I dragged him away.

The blond girl giggled and waved. Her dark-haired friend rolled her eyes.

"Dorks," she muttered.

The third girl, the one with the reddish hair, just watched us go. She looked amused.

"What's the big idea?" Joe finally broke free of my grip. He looked around for the girls, but they'd already been swallowed up in the crowd. "Those three looked suspicious. I was just going to question them a little."

"Yeah, right." I let out a snort. "Get your hormones under control, Mr. Slick. We've got work to do."

Joe snapped to attention and saluted. "Sir, yes sir!"

Just then there was a commotion up ahead. A camera crew was emerging from the backstage area. They were surrounding a gorgeous young woman holding a microphone. I recognized her as Annie Wu, a VJ from the music television station. Fans were pushing forward, trying to catch a better look at the VJ. As soon as the crew was through, the guards returned to their positions in front of the backstage gate.

"We really need to get in there," Joe said. "Let's see if we can find a weak spot in the fence."

At least he was back on track with the mission. "Okay," I said. "Can't hurt to check it out."

I still wasn't sure trying to sneak in was the best use of our time right then. But at least it would distract Joe from girls for a few minutes.

Less than ten minutes later we were in. It wasn't even a challenge to our ATAC skills—we just walked along the fence until we came to a spot where two sections of the fence came together. Or rather, where they *didn't* come together. They were hooked to each other with a chain, but there was a space between them just big enough for us to squeeze through. There was a green-shirted guard nearby, but he was talking on a cell phone with his back to us, so we got through easily.

Once we were inside, nobody paid any attention to us. There were tons of people running around, looking busy and important. We started walking, taking in the whole scene.

"Look," I said. "That must be the official press area."

There were a bunch of big portable lights set up around a small stage containing a couple of director's chairs with the Rockapazooma logo on them. A neon green screen stood behind the stage.

Joe glanced that way and nodded. "Guess nobody's getting interviewed right now," he said. "Come on, let's check out the band trailers."

We wandered deeper into the backstage area. Trailers, buses, and semis loomed all around us. There were fewer people walking around in this section, although there were big, muscular guys guarding some of the trailers and buses.

After turning a corner we passed a large but nondescript trailer. Just ahead I noticed a cotton-candy pink tour bus painted with airy white swirls.

"Wonder which band came in that thing?" I said.

"Bet it wasn't DJ Razz." Joe grinned. "If he was seen in a bus like that, his fans would disown him."

I laughed. "Yeah, but what better way to travel incognito?" I said. "Nobody would ever guess Razz was inside that Barbie-doll-looking thing."

"True." Joe glanced over at the generic-looking trailer we were passing at the moment. "But I still bet he'd rather—"

Joe was cut off by a sudden, bloodcurdling scream.

NANCY

CHAPTER 4

CHANCE ENCOUNTERS

Ned had to be at the concert early. Bess, George, and I weren't complaining about that. We were so psyched to be at Rockapazooma that we were all about to burst.

"I need to go sign in at the press tent," Ned told us after we cleared the metal detector at the entrance gate. "Want to come along? I can try to get you guys backstage with me."

"Awesome!" George's eyes sparkled. "Maybe we'll see Nick Needles or Mike Manslaughter walking around!"

"Mike Manslaughter?" Bess wrinkled her nose. "Let me guess—another member of Lethal Injection?"

"Duh. He's only the lead singer." George tugged on Ned's arm. "Come on, let's go!"

We wound our way through the crowd. I couldn't believe it was already so packed. The show wouldn't start for almost ninety minutes, but it looked as if at least half of the expected 200,000 people were already there. Some people had set up folding chairs in front of the stage, while others were lying out in the sun on picnic blankets or tossing Frisbees or playing Hacky Sack. There were long lines at the refreshment stands and the souvenir booths, and even longer ones at the restrooms.

"Wow," I said. "This is wild! I can't believe we're really here."

Ned reached over and squeezed my hand. "Having fun so far?"

"Definitely." I smiled and squeezed back. "I just can't believe how crowded it is. Good thing we brought cell phones in case we get separated. Because there's no way you could ever find someone in this . . ."

My voice trailed off as I spotted the backstage gate, which was just a few yards ahead now. Was I seeing things?

"What's wrong?" Ned asked.

Bess blinked. "Is that Deirdre?" she exclaimed.

There was no mistaking it. A line of security guards dressed in neon green shirts with the concert logo on them were standing in front of the gate. Deirdre was glaring up at one of them, a man approximately the same size and shape as a refrigerator. He stared at her impassively, his meaty arms crossed over his chest. I guessed that his green T-shirt had to be a size XXXL.

"Oh, man," George muttered, staring at Deirdre in disbelief. "We've been here twenty minutes, and look who we run into. What are the odds?"

I shook my head. "I don't know. But it looks like maybe that backstage pass of hers isn't working too well."

We hurried forward. Deirdre was waving her hands around and whining at the huge guard. Now that we were closer, I could see that the name tag pinned to the guard's shirt identified him as TYREESE—SECURITY.

". . . and if you had more than two brain cells to rub together, you'd realize that I'm obviously telling the truth," Deirdre was complaining as we got close enough to overhear. "I was told quite clearly that this ticket gives me free admission to the *entire* concert grounds. And that obviously means I should be able to go backstage without some oversized rent-a-guard stopping me, and . . ."

As we all listened in, George's expression changed from annoyance to delight. Finally she stepped forward.

"Well, hello, DeeDee," she said. "Having some problems, are we?"

Deirdre spun around, looking startled. "Oh, it's you," she spat. "Mind your own business. I'm just trying to explain to this doofus that I need to get backstage." She spun around to glare at the guard again. "Just wait until my friends Kijani and Nicky Needles hear about this. Oh, and Toni Lovely, too. They're all close friends of mine, you know. Did you hear me? Once my good friend Kijani hears about this, you'll never work security in this town again!"

The guard didn't look impressed by her threat. "Nobody gets backstage without the proper authorization," he rumbled in a deep voice. "Not without going through me first."

Ned shot me an amused glance. "Maybe this isn't the best time to try to get you guys backstage after all," he murmured.

George heard the guard too. She looked disappointed, but she nodded. "We'll have to meet up with you later."

"Definitely." Ned patted the cell phone clipped to his belt. "See you."

He stepped past Deirdre, who was still ranting at the top of her lungs. Approaching one of the other guards, Ned held up his press pass. The guard peered at it, then waved him through.

"See you, Ned!" George sang out loudly, waving at him. "Have fun backstage!"

Deirdre heard and shot her a dirty look. George smiled pleasantly in return. "You too, Deirdre," she said sweetly. "*If* you ever get back there, that is."

Bess grabbed her by the arm and dragged her away.

"Come on," she chided with a smile. "Stop teasing Deirdre. It's not nice."

"Says who?" George grinned.

Just then I noticed a guy around our age charging toward us. He was cute, with wavy blond hair and blue eyes. "Who's that?" I asked my friends. "Someone you know?"

Bess and George both shook their heads. "Looks like he wants to know us, though," George commented. "*One* of us, anyway."

As he got closer, it became obvious that the blond guy was staring at Bess. That was nothing new. With her blond hair, great figure, and dimples, Bess turns heads wherever she goes. Guys are always coming up to her on the street, in restaurants, at the mall, in the post office—pretty much anywhere. Luckily Bess never lets all the attention go to her head. In fact, she kind of hates it.

The guy skidded to a stop in front of us. "Hi," he said breathlessly, his eyes locked on to Bess. "I'm Joe. What's your—"

"Excuse us."

Another guy had suddenly appeared. He was a little taller and leaner than the blond guy, but just as good-looking, with dark hair and an intense expression on his angular face. Without another word, he grabbed the first guy's arm and yanked him away.

Bess giggled and waved as the two guys moved away.

"Dorks," George muttered, rolling her eyes.

I just watched in amusement as the blond guy struggled against his friend's grip. "Too bad, Bess," I commented as the two guys were lost behind a group of teenagers batting around a beach ball. "Those guys were pretty cute."

Just then Deirdre's voice floated toward us from back by the gate. "Fine!" she shrieked. "You win, okay? But this isn't the last you've seen of me! As soon as I get in touch with Kijani and Nick, I'll be back!"

I glanced over that way just in time to see Deirdre storm off, her face frozen in a furious scowl. She pushed between a couple of the beach-ball-tossing teens.

"Yo!" one of them said in surprise. "Watch it!"

"Watch it yourself," Deirdre snarled, not slowing her pace as she stalked off into the crowd.

"Come on." George was already heading off after her. "If her head's about to explode, I want to be there to see it."

I had to admit I was at least mildly curious about what Deirdre would do next. As I've already mentioned, she isn't the type to give up easily on something she wants.

"Okay, why not," I said. "We still have a while until the concert starts."

"Oh, Nancy." Bess sounded amused. "You'll do anything to pretend you have a mystery to solve."

I shrugged and grinned. "You're right," I told Bess with a smile. "It's the mystery of how Deirdre Shannon is going to enjoy herself at this concert if she can't get backstage to rub elbows with the stars."

George gestured to us impatiently. "Hurry up—we're losing her!"

Even in the ever-growing crowd it wasn't too difficult to keep track of Deirdre. All we had to do was follow the chorus of *Hey*s and *Watch it*s and *Ow*s she left in her wake as she rudely pushed past people. It also helped that she was wearing a hot pink shirt with yellow trim. Deirdre likes to stand out.

We stayed back a few yards, trying not to let her see us while keeping her in sight. As we walked, we also had a chance to look around and to see more of the concert area.

Deirdre's path was leading us deeper into the crowd in front of the stage, which had grown thicker as the concert's start time drew closer. People were sitting, standing, dancing, or wandering across the field. Here and there we could see the bright green of a security guard's T-shirt among them. Up on the stage, workers were setting up microphones and busily moving equipment back and forth. The atmosphere, which had been relaxed when we arrived, was sizzling with anticipation.

"Hey, look!" Bess said, pointing as one of the video screens hanging over the huge stage flickered to life. It showed the Rockapazooma logo for a moment or two, then started flashing images of trees, wildlife, oceans, and other scenes of nature.

"Almost time!" George had to raise her voice to be heard over the buzz of conversation, laughter, and random outbursts of singing all around us.

I glanced ahead, catching a glimpse of Deirdre's pink shirt. She had just passed the nearest large speaker tower, which was located in the middle of the front section of the audience area about fifty yards from the stage. Judging by the direction she was going, I guessed she was heading for the line of refreshment stands off to the left side of the stage area.

"Maybe we should start looking for a spot to watch from," Bess suggested. "It looks like we're losing Deirdre anyway."

Turning to glance once more toward the speaker tower, I saw that she was right. Deirdre had disappeared behind a cluster of middle-aged men who were tossing around a football.

"Okay," I said. "Where do you want to go?"

Bess opened her mouth, but her answer was drowned out as the speakers suddenly crackled to life. There was a burst of music, then a voice: "Testing, testing—earth, air, sea . . ."

The crowd reacted immediately, letting out an excited roar. All around us, people surged forward, everyone trying to get closer to the stage.

Bess grabbed my hand. "Come on!" she yelled. "Let's go this way!"

I nodded and started to follow. But something made me glance over toward that speaker tower again—the last place I'd seen Deirdre. At that moment several of the middle-aged men tackled one of their friends, and I could see past them to the base of the metal tower.

There was a flash of hot pink. Deirdre?

"Come on, Nancy!" George shouted in my ear, giving me a shove.

"Wait!" I said, though I doubted anyone could hear me—the speakers had just emitted another ear-shattering burst of music.

But I yanked free of Bess's hand, straining to see through the crowd. There it was again—the flash of pink.

I gasped. It *was* Deirdre . . . and she was shrieking and struggling as an enormous man in a green security T-shirt roughly dragged her off.

CHAPTER 5

JOE

SEEING STARS

AAAAAAHHHHHHHHHHH!

Another hair-raising scream drifted out of the boring-looking trailer beside us. It sounded like someone inside was being stabbed, strangled, and attacked by a tiger all at the same time.

"Let's go!" I cried.

I leaped up the trailer's steps in a single bound and slammed into the door. I was expecting it to be locked, but it popped open easily. Frank was right behind me as I stumbled over the threshold.

The inside of the trailer looked nothing like the generic outside. The walls were painted bloodred, and the tile floor was black, along with all the furniture. Straight ahead of me was a poster of a guy about to have his head chopped off by a hooded executioner, and a full suit of medieval armor stood in the corner nearby. Weird reddish lighting cast a strange glow over the whole scene.

But I wasn't really looking at any of that stuff. I was staring at a skinny young guy with a receding hairline. He was holding up a large knife with a deadly-looking curved blade, getting ready to plunge it into another man huddled on the floor at his feet.

"Stop!" I shouted, jumping forward.

"Oy! Who are you?" the guy with the knife yelped in a British accent.

I grabbed his arm, knocking the knife onto the floor. As I twisted the dude's arm behind his back, the knife landed on the hard linoleum floor . . . and bounced.

Huh?

"Let go of me, you bloody fool!" the guy yelled, struggling against my hold.

He had a husky, squeaky sort of voice. It sounded familiar. *Really* familiar.

"Hey!" I released my grip on him. "Aren't you Mike Manslaughter from Lethal Injection?"

The guy yanked himself free and rubbed his arms. "Who else would I be?" he exclaimed, sounding irritated. "If you wanted a bloody autograph, breaking my arm wasn't the way to get it."

The second man was standing up by now. He walked

over and picked up the knife, which apparently was made of rubber.

Oops.

"Joe," Frank said from behind me, "I think there's been a little misunderstanding here."

That's my brother—Captain Obvious.

"I'm so sorry," I told both guys, feeling like the world's biggest idiot. By now, I'd recognized the second guy as Nick Needles, the band's drummer. "I totally didn't recognize you at first. You know, without the makeup."

It was true. It's amazing how different a guy can look when he's not wearing acid yellow makeup, a shaggy purple fright wig, and a leather bodysuit. With his pasty face and receding brown hair, dressed in jeans and a T-shirt, Mike Manslaughter looked like an ordinary guy. An *angry* ordinary guy.

"So you're saying if you recognized us, you wouldn't have barged in here and attacked us?" he said, his voice dripping with sarcasm. "I'm calling security."

"Please don't!" Frank said. "We didn't mean to bother you. We heard you screaming, and thought you were in trouble."

"Right," I added. "We were just trying to help."

I was a little distracted. Now that I knew we were in Lethal Injection's trailer, I couldn't help looking around. The place was packed with weird stuff. In addition to the suit of armor, there were all kinds of funky weapons hanging on the walls—scimitars, crossbows, stuff like that. In one corner was a glass case that held even more weapons, from grenades to brass knuckles to bayonets. A pile of cannonballs sat near the doorway, and a rope noose hung from the light fixture overhead.

"Hold on, Mikey." Nick Needles sounded a lot calmer than his bandmate. "Who are you two, anyway?"

We introduced ourselves as Jimmy and Jack Leyland. "I'm your biggest fan," I added.

Mike Manslaughter rolled his eyes. "*Now* the truth comes out," he said. "Call the guards, Nick. These two are probably those bloggers who vowed to unveil our murder scenario before the show."

Okay, call me slow. But it wasn't until he said that that I realized what we'd just interrupted.

"Wow!" I exclaimed. "So *that* was tonight's murder you guys were practicing? Sweet!"

Mike Manslaughter twisted his face into a threatening scowl. It looked almost as scary as his stage makeup.

But Nick Needles merely shrugged. "You got it, mates," he told us. "Mikey and I like to rehearse a few times throughout the day. It's a good way to psyche ourselves up for the performance. The rest of the guys will join us for a couple of final rehearsals later."

"Awesome!" I could hardly believe we'd witnessed

the next Lethal Injection death scene. I'd heard the band didn't even let their agent in on the secret beforehand.

"I hope you enjoy it while you're sitting in the local jailhouse for the rest of the day," Mike Manslaughter said, sounding much less friendly than Nick. "Because there's no way we're going to let you loose to ruin the secret."

Uh-oh. We couldn't let that happen. No way. If Frank and I got dragged off to the police station, how were we supposed to complete our mission? Sure, we could call ATAC HQ and get ourselves released. But by the time we got back here, who knows how much we would have missed?

My hand strayed toward my jeans pocket. The mini-cattle-prod device was in there. If I could get it out and stun both band members, it should give us enough time to escape. I decided to go for Nick Needles first—he was a lot bigger and stronger-looking.

"I have to tell you," Frank said, "I really admire you guys."

I was so startled that I froze with my hand halfway into my pocket. Since when was Frank a Lethal Injection fan?

"Thanks," Nick Needles said, and Mike Manslaughter grunted.

"No, I mean it!" Frank had his superearnest Eagle

Scout face on. Even more than usual, I mean. "Your band is totally brilliant in the way you meld early metal influences with current hardcore riffs and the best of the old glam rock style. And don't even get me started on how cool it is that you're so dedicated to the environment—that's totally awesome. My brother and I are really into that stuff too."

"Really?" Mike Manslaughter looked suspicious. But he sounded a fraction less hostile. "How so?"

As for me, I was still surprised that Frank knew all that stuff about LI's music. But I had also figured out what he was doing. It's true what they say—flattery will get you everywhere. But I kept my hand near my jeans pocket just in case.

"Oh, we love the environment," I said. "We're always looking for ways to help out the cause. Right, bro?"

Frank nodded. "That's why we were so psyched to get tickets for Rockapazooma," he said. "Well, that and the fact that some of our favorite bands would be here, like you guys."

"You're too kind." Nick Needles smiled at us.

But Mike Manslaughter still didn't seem totally convinced. "Yeah, that's nice and all," he said. "Almost makes me sorry to call the cops on you two. But we gotta protect our secret."

"I understand." Frank looked so earnest by now that I was ready to nominate him for sainthood myself. "But if you let us go, we swear we won't tell anyone what we just saw. We can keep a secret."

"Totally," I said. "We wouldn't want to ruin the surprise for the other fans, anyway."

"That's a good point." Nick Needles glanced at his bandmate. "Come on, Mikey, lighten up. These kids don't seem like the blabbermouth type."

"We're not!" I said. "We're so totally, totally not."

It took a few more minutes of convincing them that we wouldn't tell in order to get them to let us off the hook. In the end Mike Manslaughter actually made us swear on this giant stage-prop fake Bible he got from the back room. But finally they agreed to let us go.

"Thanks, guys," Frank said. "We won't let you down."

"You'd better not," Mike Manslaughter growled. "I'm writing down your names just in case. Jimmy and Jack Leyland."

Yeah, a lot of good that will do you.

"Come on, Jimmy," Frank said. "Let's go leave these guys alone."

"Right behind you." I paused just before reaching the door. "It was awesome meeting you guys! Rock on!"

Outside, we raced out of sight around the corner before collapsing against another trailer in relief.

"Whew!" I said. "That was a close one."

Frank checked his watch. "It's getting close to show-time," he said. "Maybe we should—"

"Hey! You two!"

I looked up. One of the biggest guys I've ever seen was lumbering toward us. He was wearing one of those bright-green planet T-shirts.

"Uh-oh," I said. "Guard!"

Frank and I took off at a run, but that guard moved fast for such a big guy. I'd barely gone three steps when I felt him grab my shoulder. Talk about a strong grip—it was like getting snagged by one of those machines that lift and crush old cars.

He spun us both around. "IDs, boys?" he rumbled.

Frank cleared his throat and peered up at the guy's name tag. "Hi there, uh, Tyreese, sir," he said. "We seem to have misplaced our backstage passes, but—"

The guard didn't let him finish. "You'll have to come with me."

Just then there was a burst of talk and laughter from around the corner ahead. A group of people came into sight a second later. Most of them were huge bodyguard types or dudes in suits. But in the middle was a girl.

My eyes widened as I recognized her. "Kijani!" I blurted.

She looked over at me and smiled. That made me forget all about the guard's bear-paw-like hand crushing my shoulder. It made me forget that Frank and I were about to be kicked out of the backstage area, if not the concert itself.

It practically made me forget my own name.

Kijani was even more incredible in person than she was on TV. She had springy black hair and smooth, cocoa-tinted skin. Until that moment, I hadn't known that one girl could look so amazing.

"Hello there," she said in a musical accent. "What is going on here, my friends?"

Our buddy Tyreese cleared his throat. It sounded like a volcano getting ready to erupt.

"Nothing to worry about, Ms. Kijani," he said. "I was just removing these intruders."

I barely heard him. I was still too busy staring.

"I'm your biggest fan, Kijani!" I blurted out, hardly believing that was really her standing in front of me. "Do you mind if I call you Kijani? Seriously, you're the greatest—I don't usually even like top forty stuff all that much, but I play your CD all the time, and . . ."

I'm not even sure what else I said. All I was aware of was that she was looking at me. *Me*, Joe Hardy. Being looked at by Kijani. Why wasn't there a camera crew around when I needed one? Because there was no *way* my friends back home were going to believe me when I told them about this!

"Aren't you sweet," she said with a smile. She gestured to Tyreese. "Sir, these two surely are not doing any harm. Perhaps you could let them go?"

"But, Ms.—" Tyreese began, sounding stubborn.

"Sir." One of Kijani's companions stepped forward. She was a tall, skinny white woman in a business suit. Her whole look and attitude practically screamed *publicist*. "I'm sure these boys are just overeager fans. It would make Kijani happy to see them free to enjoy the show."

"Please?" Kijani smiled up at the guard.

I almost felt bad for poor Tyreese. What was he supposed to say to that?

"Fine," he grumbled, releasing his iron grip on Frank and me. He glared at us threateningly. "But if I catch you boys back here again . . ."

"Don't worry, you won't," Frank assured him quickly, rubbing his shoulder.

"Come on," the publicist lady said, putting a hand on Kijani's shoulder. "The TV folks from Washington are waiting."

Kijani nodded. "See you, guys," she said, waving to me and Frank. "Enjoy the concert." Then she hurried off with her posse.

I stared after her, but Frank grabbed me and dragged me off toward the gate, and back out into the concert area. Tyreese glared after us.

Soon we were out mixing with the crowd again. It was kind of a letdown after our brushes with the stars backstage.

"Okay," I said to Frank. "Now what?"

Frank shrugged. "Back to work."

We started off through the crowd. There were a lot more people out there than there had been a little while ago. We stepped in front of the stage just in time to hear the giant speakers all over the grounds burst into action. "Testing, testing—earth, air, sea . . ."

CHAPTER 6

NANCY

SHOWTIME

"Wait!" I yelled to my friends. "Look, it's Deirdre. I think she's in trouble!"

The crowd had shifted again, hiding Deirdre and her green-shirted captor from view. Luckily, after one last burst of static, the speakers quieted down again.

"What did you say, Nancy?" Bess asked, swaying and grabbing my arm as a bunch of excited-looking tweens bumped into her while racing past on their way toward the stage.

"I just saw Deirdre over there." I pointed toward the speaker tower. "Some big guy in one of those security T-shirts was pushing her over toward the stage."

"Good," George said. "Sounds like she managed to get herself kicked out."

I hesitated, glancing once more toward where I'd seen the scuffle. Was George right? I wasn't so sure. There was something about the rough way the man had been yanking Deirdre along. . . .

"Things didn't look quite right," I said. "Deirdre looked pretty upset."

Bess shrugged. "What would upset her more than getting kicked out of this concert after bragging about her backstage passes to everyone she knows?"

"I know. But I have a hunch. . . ."

Bess and George groaned and exchanged a glance. But they didn't say anything. They know my hunches are usually right.

"Come on," I said, hoping it wasn't already too late to catch up to Deirdre and the guard. "Let's go check it out."

It wasn't easy getting through the crowd, which had swelled since the speakers had come on. Leading the way, I pushed past a bunch of rowdy college guys and the middle-aged men with the football, and finally reached a relatively open area near the base of the big speaker tower.

"There they are!" I shouted, pointing.

Deirdre and the green-shirted man were a dozen yards ahead. He had a firm grip on both her elbows, which he was twisting behind her back in an uncomfortable-looking way. Deirdre was screaming at the top of her lungs, earning annoyed, confused, and concerned glances from the people around her. But nobody seemed willing to confront the guard.

"Deirdre!" I yelled.

Not waiting for my friends, I raced toward them. The guard turned and spotted me.

He was big—almost as big as that guard who'd turned Deirdre away from the backstage gate. Muscles bulged beneath his neon green T-shirt, and his broad face wore a grim expression. But what caught my eye was the scar. The man's bald head, like the rest of his skin, was the dark brown hue of burnished mahogany. Standing out against it was a jagged, raised white line, a good eight inches long. It started in the middle of his forehead and angled up across the left side of his skull. What could cause that kind of scar?

But that was beside the point at the moment. "Excuse me . . ." I tore my gaze away from the hideous scar and searched for the man's name tag, but he wasn't wearing one. "Um, sir," I went on. "Is there a problem here? I know this girl."

Deirdre had finally spotted me. "Nancy!" she gasped. "Tell this goon to let me go. Just wait until my father hears about this—never mind what my dear friend Kijani will say . . ."

"Shut up, Deirdre," I told her.

Just then Bess and George finally caught up. "What's going on?" George panted.

"I'm not sure." I stared at the guard, who still hadn't spoken a word. "That's what I was just asking this man."

"Yo! Blondie!"

I glanced over my shoulder. Three or four of the college boys I'd passed a second ago were rushing toward us. All of them were gazing eagerly at Bess. They were big and well-fed and athletic-looking guys, all wearing matching fraternity T-shirts.

Deirdre spotted them too. "Help me!" she shrieked, wriggling more vigorously than ever against her captor. "Please! I didn't do anything wrong."

The guys looked toward her. "Dude!" one of them exclaimed. "Is that any way to treat a lady?"

"Especially a hot one like that," a second guy added.

"Look," I began. "Let's all just settle down, and . . ."

Before I could finish, the guard suddenly shoved Deirdre forward. She stumbled into me, almost knocking me to the ground. As one of the frat boys stepped forward just in time to catch us, I saw the guard turn and take off into the crowd.

"Hey!" I shouted.

"Easy, babe," the frat guy said, tightening his grip around my waist. "I've got you."

I pushed him away. "Let me go!"

"Hey, stop poking me!"

I'd nearly forgotten that Deirdre was still collapsed

against me. She tried to straighten up by clawing at my shoulders and pushing against me for balance. I found myself spitting out strands of her dark hair, and for a few seconds I couldn't really see what was happening. By the time I got clear of both her and the frat guy, there was no sign of the runaway guard.

"Which way did he go?" I asked Bess and George.

"I'm not sure," George said. "He ran off that way, but I lost sight of him in the crowd."

"Come on, maybe we can still catch up." I took a few steps in the direction George had pointed, but found my way blocked by two more frat guys. Their number seemed to be growing all the time.

"Hey, meathead, let us through!" George exclaimed, pushing at one of them, a beefy guy with a blond buzz cut and an amiable expression.

He grinned. "Whoa, check out this chick," he said. "Didn't mean to get in your way, babe."

"Don't call me that," George growled.

I tried to dodge around the guys, but there were too many of them. Meanwhile Deirdre was complaining loudly as several of the guys hovered around her nearby.

". . . and as soon as Kijani hears about this, she'll have that guy fired!" she screeched at the top of her lungs. "Just wait and see! I'm going to complain to the management right now. They'll be lucky if I don't have my father sue them out of business."

"I'll come with you, babe," one of the frat guys told Deirdre. "I'm, like, a witness."

Deirdre tossed her head and looked him over. Then she turned and pointed to another guy. I couldn't help noticing that he was the best-looking of the bunch.

"You," she said. "You're a witness. Want to help me report what that jerk did to me?"

"Sure!" the cute guy said. "Come on, let's go."

"You're welcome," I murmured as I watched Deirdre prance off on the frat guy's arm. Most of the other frat guys trailed along after them, though two or three lingered behind and continued to ogle Bess.

Bess ignored them, shooting me a sympathetic look. "You'd think even Deirdre might thank you for scaring off that goon."

Just then there was a sudden increase in noise from the crowd nearby. I glanced over, hoping to spot the guard with the scar. Instead I saw a camera crew making their way through the hordes of people. At the center of the group of camera operators and lighting guys, I spotted a familiar face.

"Isn't that Annie Wu?" George sounded excited. "She's that VJ from the music channel!"

I nodded, too distracted by what had just happened to care much about a minor celebrity spotting. But Bess and George, along with the leftover frat guys, were already surging forward to meet the camera crew.

"Hi there, people!" Annie Wu cried out in her high-pitched, peppy voice. "We're looking for a few of you music fans to say some words about today's cause—environmental protection. Who has something fun to say about it? How about you girls?"

To my surprise, she pointed directly at my friends and me. *Great,* I thought, craning my neck to see past them into the crowd where the guard had disappeared. *We really don't have time for this.*

But George was nodding eagerly. "Sure!" she said. "We'd love to say a few words. Right, guys?"

Bess was nodding too. Before I could say anything, someone shoved me hard in the back. I stumbled forward, then glanced over to see Deirdre barging past me. A couple of the frat guys were right behind her.

"Excuse me!" she said loudly. "Did you say you want to interview a music fan? I'm a huge music fan. I'd better be, considering Kijani herself is a close friend, not to mention Nick Needles." She laughed loudly and patted her hair. "Is this going to be aired on TV?"

"Maybe later," Annie Wu answered, looking slightly confused. "But we're mainly taping these segments to be shown on the big screens later. You know—between acts."

"Oh. I guess that's okay too." Deirdre shrugged. "So, interview away. I'm ready."

"Hey, wait a minute," George began, sounding annoyed.

Before she could say any more, I grabbed her and yanked her away. Bess followed.

"Come on," I said. "This is our chance to escape!"

"Escape?" George was still glaring at Deirdre. The camera operators were taking their positions as she slicked on a layer of lip gloss. "Why would we want to do that?"

I glanced over as Deirdre's interview began. We were a little too far away to hear everything she was saying, although I did catch her dropping Kijani's name several times. No surprise there.

"Yeah, what's the rush?" Bess asked me. "That scar guy is long gone by now."

I had to admit she was right about that. It was way too late to try following that guy through the crowd.

"I know," I said. "But I think we need to figure out what he was trying to do."

"Wait a minute." George turned and stared at me. "Are you trying to turn Deirdre getting herself kicked out for general obnoxiousness into some kind of deeper mystery?"

I shrugged, smiling sheepishly. "You've got to admit, it didn't look quite right. You know, the way he grabbed her, and then took off as soon as he was challenged."

"Yeah. It *is* pretty suspicious that anyone would want to touch Deirdre," George said.

Bess giggled. "You know our Nancy," she told George. "She finds mysteries everywhere she—"

"GOOD MORNING, MUSIC FANS!"

We were still standing right beneath that big speaker tower, so when the sound system burst to life again, it made us all jump.

It also made further conversation pretty much impossible. I turned to face the stage as everyone around me starting cheering, whistling, and stomping their feet.

"WELCOME TO ROCKAPAZOOMA!" the speakers howled. *"AND NOW GIVE A BIG SHOUT-OUT FOR YOUR HOST, MACK-DADDY McMILLAN!"*

The cheering grew as a skinny, wild-haired man jogged onto the stage, pumping his fists in the air and whooping. Mack-Daddy McMillan was a popular DJ from the local rock station. Any further thoughts about Deirdre or the guy with the scar fled my mind immediately. I gave in to the excitement all around me, raised both hands over my head, and screamed at the top of my lungs.

The concert had begun!

CHAPTER 7

FRANK

ALL TALK, NO ACTION?

". . . NOW GIVE A BIG SHOUT-OUT FOR YOUR HOST, MACK-DADDY McMILLAN!"

Beside me, Joe let out a whoop and pumped his fist in the air. "Go, Mack-Daddy!"

"Come on." I yanked him along after me. We were hurrying through the crowd near the right edge of the stage. We'd spent the last few minutes exploring the open, alley-type area between the stage and the trailer area, which was populated mostly by roadies, techs, and guys who were too desperate to wait in line at the restrooms.

Other than the smell, nothing back there seemed out of the ordinary. The more time passed, the more I wondered exactly what we were supposed to be doing. So far we'd seen plenty of underage drinking, and a few other illegal acts. But none of it seemed ATAC-worthy.

Now the show was about to start, and we were no closer to knowing why we were there. Talk about frustrating!

What if this mission is all about ticket scalping? I thought. *Maybe we should have stayed out by the gate a little longer to see if anything was going down out there.*

The emcee grabbed the mike and introduced himself as a DJ from a local radio station. "I'll be here all day, grooving to the music right along with you," he said, his voice amplified through the dozens of huge speakers. "I hope you're as stoked as I am! We've got thirteen awesome acts here to perform for you. All of them are donating their time and talents for the cause of environmental protection. Let's give them a hand for that!"

The crowd whooped their appreciation. Joe stuck two fingers in his mouth and let out a piercing whistle.

But I was only half listening. *Why couldn't the ATAC guys tell us a little more about those theories they have?* I wondered. *Maybe then we wouldn't be wandering around wasting time, trying to figure it out on our own.*

"A lot of these bands have been working for the cause for a long time," Mack-Daddy went on. "For instance, one of our headliners, Lethal Injection . . ."

He had to pause as the crowd went wild at the

mention of the band's name. Joe added to the din, jumping up and down and shouting.

Meanwhile I was looking around, trying to figure out what to do next. I realized we hadn't checked out the food and souvenir stands yet, and that area was only going to get more crowded.

From where I was standing, I could barely see the tops of the temporary food and gift stalls over the heads of the crowd. The shopping area was all the way on the other side of the place, beginning about fifty yards from the speaker tower at the left edge of the stage, and stretching back as far as I could see.

". . . and so that's why they signed on as soon as they heard about this concert," Mack-Daddy was saying, after listing some of Lethal Injection's environmental creds. "They even postponed their tour of Sweden to be here. Too bad for all those metalheads in Stockholm!"

The audience laughed and cheered again. Mack-Daddy grinned and raised his hands for quiet.

"And then there's everybody's favorite hip-hop artist, and another longtime friend of the environmental movement," he said. "Of course, you all know I have to be talking about the one and only DJ Razz. . . ."

I shaded my eyes, gauging how long it would take us to push through the crowd in front of the stage. Then I nudged Joe.

"Hey." I had to lean close enough to speak directly

into his ear. Otherwise there was no way he could have heard me. "Let's duck back there again."

I gestured back the way we'd come. Joe shot me a look of disbelief.

"But the show's about to start!" he yelled.

"Come on." I grabbed his arm and pulled him along with me.

It was a little quieter behind the stage, since all the speakers were pointing out the other way. But we could still easily hear the DJ.

". . . and Razz might not be afraid to mess with the law," he was saying. "But he has the utmost respect for the laws of nature . . ."

"What's the big idea?" Joe demanded. "I was watching!"

"We're not here to watch. We're here to work. And I think we should finish checking out the whole site, starting with the food stalls."

"Fine." Joe shrugged. "I could use a drink anyway."

We hurried along the back of the stage. A couple of roadies shot us suspicious looks, but nobody tried to stop us or ask us what we were doing back there. A bunch of green-shirted security guards were standing near the spot where people had to cross over from the backstage trailer area, which was blocked off by more chain-link, to the actual back of the stage. But no celebrities were trying to pass through at the moment, so they waved us across.

Meanwhile, the DJ's spiel continued out front. ". . . and if you've never seen the Rotten Punks perform live, you're in for a good time today. Then we have the Bootstraps all the way from Ireland, and talented young homegrown singer-songwriter Toni Lovely, and dance sensation Cherry Pye . . ."

Joe and I rounded the corner and looked out at the crowd again. If anything, it was even more packed on this side of the stage. I shaded my eyes and glanced at the food stands. They looked crowded too.

"Let's wait until the music starts," I said into Joe's ear. "People will probably forget about buying food and come out to watch."

"Whatever."

". . . and then there's our other big headliner, the Royal We," Mack-Daddy was saying. This time he had to stop for at least twenty seconds until the cheers died down. "As you all know by now, the lovely and talented lead singer of the band, Kijani, is a member of the deposed royal family of Urdzania. She and her parents barely escaped with their lives when a ruthless dictator staged a coup and took over the country."

"Yeah, they were totally lucky," I commented. "The guy who took over Urdzania is brutal. He once had a guy's head chopped off with a machete for serving him the wrong soup."

Joe shot me a surprised look. "Hold on. A week ago

you'd barely heard of the Royal We. Now you're an expert on the history of Kijani's country?"

"Research." I shrugged. "You should try it sometime."

Joe rolled his eyes. I grinned. It drives him crazy that I'm so much more thorough than he is. Don't get me wrong—I love the action and danger and excitement of our missions just as much as he does. But I also love the challenge of figuring out how all the pieces fit together. Over the past week, I'd researched every band on the bill today, as well as the producers, the environmental groups involved, and anyone else who had anything to do with the show.

". . . and when she's not speaking out against what's happening in her homeland, Kijani puts tons of energy into the cause of environmental protection," MackDaddy was saying. "It's a passion she inherited from her parents, who were among the first rulers in that part of Africa to take conservation to the next level, and . . ."

"Is this guy ever going to shut up?" Joe commented. "We came to hear music, not listen to him blab."

An older guy with a long, grayish-brown ponytail heard him and laughed. "Right on, dude!" he said, giving Joe a thumbs-up. Joe grinned and returned the gesture.

The DJ said a few more words about a few of the other acts. "Okay, but enough yapping from me," he said. "Who wants to hear some music?"

The crowd roared. Joe reached out to high-five the ponytail guy.

"All right!" Up onstage Mack-Daddy grinned out at the audience. "Then without further ado, I give you the talented and oh-so-lovely Toni Lovely! Let's make her feel welcome, people!"

There were plenty of cheers and shouts and whistles from all around us, but Joe looked less than thrilled.

"Toni Lovely?" he said. "Isn't that the chick who sings about clouds and stuff?"

I hoped his lack of enthusiasm meant he would be able to focus on the mission for a while. Joe can be Mr. Short Attention Span at the best of times. But being at the big concert seemed to be distracting him way more than usual.

"Yeah," I told him. "She even has a song about a dying goose. I think it's supposed to be a metaphor or something."

Joe let out a snort. "Was that part of your research too? Or are you a closet Toni Lovely fan?"

I didn't rise to the bait. "So what should we do?" I asked. "Check out the food stands now, or stay here and watch the crowd for a while?"

Just then there were more cheers from all around us. Glancing toward the stage, I saw Toni Lovely gliding across the floorboards. She was a pretty blonde, maybe twenty-five, carrying an acoustic guitar.

Mack-Daddy kissed her on the cheek, then stepped back. Toni Lovely smiled and leaned in toward the microphone as her band took their places.

"This is a song inspired by the plight of the world's ocean creatures," she said in a soft, husky voice amplified by the speakers. "I hope you'll all sing along. . . ."

She strummed a chord on her guitar and started to sing. The song was nice, but not exactly hard-rocking material. It sounded like something you might hear in the waiting room at the dentist's office.

When I looked back at Joe, he was staring out into the audience. "Yo," he said. "I think we should go blend in with the crowd over there."

I followed his gaze. "You mean over there by those girls in bikini tops?"

He grinned. "Hey, why not? We gotta start somewhere, right?"

I sighed. Maybe he was right. It wasn't like my check-out-the-snack-bar plan was that brilliant or anything. And the girls in bikini tops *were* cute.

"Hey, check it out!" Suddenly Joe grabbed my arm.

"What is it?" I looked over. He was staring toward a different part of the crowd now, a section right in front of the middle of the stage, about ten yards back.

"Right over there," he said. "There's some kind of commotion in the crowd. See? Maybe this is what we've been waiting for!"

Now I could see what he'd seen: a ripple in the crowd, as if something was happening just out of our line of sight. But I held him back before he could take off.

"Hold it," I said. "That looks more like a spur-of-the-moment mosh pit than anything serious."

"A mosh pit? For Toni Lovely?" Joe shot a skeptical glance at the woman strumming her guitar and crooning onstage.

He had a point. "Okay," I said. "But how are we supposed to get over there?"

The thickest part of the crowd stood between here and there. Joe glanced around.

"I know how we can get a better look," he said.

He turned and darted back the way we'd come. I followed, confused.

Then he grabbed one of the metal support rods and swung himself up onto it. That's when I realized what he wanted to do.

"Climb up the speaker tower?" I said. "Are you nuts?"

He grinned. "I've been called worse." Grabbing the next bar, he glanced down at me. "Come on! If we stay toward the back, nobody out front will be able to see us. And we'll be able to see everything from up there."

I hesitated. Leave it to Joe to come up with a crazy idea like climbing up the side of the stage just to get a better view.

Then again . . .

Joe grabbed another bar. Then he paused and glanced down. "Are you coming?"

"Right behind you."

I grabbed the nearest piece of framework and started climbing.

CHAPTER 8

NANCY

A CLUE AND A CHASE

"I love this song!" Bess cried, swaying in place as Toni Lovely strummed a few chords and began the next verse of her first song.

George was singing along with her. Luckily she kept it under her breath. I love the girl, but she's totally tone-deaf.

I was enjoying Toni Lovely's performance too. But I was kind of distracted. For some reason, I couldn't stop thinking about the incident with that green-shirted security guard.

Or was he a security guard? It hadn't taken me long to notice that all the other guards were wearing name tags on their neon green shirts. The guy with the scar hadn't had one.

I bet he's a fake, I thought as Toni Lovely began her second song. *He was probably just trying to blend in so he could grab Deirdre and drag her off without arousing suspicion. But why?*

George glanced over and caught me staring off into the crowd. "Are you still looking for that thug?" she asked, raising her voice over the music. "Give it up, Nance. He's long gone by now."

"I know," I said. "I just wish I could've caught up with him."

"Don't worry about it, Nancy," Bess advised. "He was probably just a pickpocket or something."

I wasn't so sure about that. Why would a pickpocket put on a bright neon green security guard's T-shirt? It wouldn't exactly allow him to blend in with the crowd. And why would he try to drag Deirdre away? That too had only attracted more attention to himself.

Not a pickpocket, I thought. *So what was he trying to do?*

Deirdre's family is well-off, but I doubted they were wealthy enough for anybody to try to kidnap her for ransom. It could be some kind of revenge for one of her father's law cases, but why would someone try to grab her at a huge public event like Rockapazooma? It's not as if Deirdre's a hermit. All a kidnapper would have to do is hang out at the mall or in the country club parking lot for a day or two, and they could grab her there.

"Maybe it's not about Deirdre at all," I said to myself. "Maybe it was just a random crime."

"Huh?" George glanced over.

I hadn't even realized I was speaking aloud. Feeling a bit silly for speculating about such things during the concert of the decade, I decided not to share the truth. My friends already thought I was mystery-obsessed.

"Um, I said it's awfully hot out here. I think I'll go get a soda or something," I said. "Want me to bring you back something?"

"You're going now?" Bess glanced at me in surprise. "But Toni Lovely is on!"

"Don't worry, I'll still be able to hear her." I smiled, gesturing to the enormous speaker tower rising out of the crowd just a few yards away.

Soon I was pushing my way through the masses of people standing between me and the food area off to one side of the concert grounds. I hadn't gone far before it started to seem an impossible task. For one thing, I wasn't sure I was going in the right direction. I'm not particularly short, but it was difficult to see over the heads of all the taller people around me to the outskirts of the crowd where the snack bars were located.

At least I'll be able to find my way back to Bess and George, I thought, glancing over my shoulder. The central speaker tower rose like a beacon marking the area where they were standing. *Too bad there's not one of those things by the snack bars.*

Then I realized there *was* one landmark I could use to find my way—the stage itself. If I could make my way toward it, I could then follow it along to the left until I reached the far edge, which was close to where the food stands began. It certainly wasn't the shortest route to the soda stand, but at least it would keep me from wandering around in circles.

I headed that way. Unfortunately it hadn't occurred to me that the crowd would get denser the closer I got to the stage. Before long I found myself in much closer contact with my fellow concertgoers than I would have preferred.

"Hey, baby," a grinning guy with mirrored shades said as I squeezed past him.

"Excuse me," I muttered, blushing slightly as I quickly wedged myself between a pair of portly middle-aged women to get away from him.

This plan wasn't working too well. When I saw a flash of neon green ahead, I sighed in relief. A security guard. Maybe he could help me find my way over to the food stands from here.

"Pardon me," I said, wriggling through a group of dancing women. "Sorry."

Finally I squeezed past a few more people and found myself standing in front of the guard, who was looking down at a cell phone in his hand. He was just as large and muscular as the rest of the security force. His face was partially hidden by the brim of the baseball cap he was wearing. The cap was stamped with the distinctive gold logo of DJ Razz.

"Excuse me, sir," I said, tapping him on one muscular forearm. "I was wondering if you could . . ." My voice trailed off with a gasp as he looked up at me and I got a good look at his face—and the end of a raised white scar bisecting his forehead. "It's you!" I blurted out without thinking.

The guy looked startled and confused. He glanced around wildly, then spun and took off in the direction of the stage, pushing his way past startled and annoyed fans.

I raced after him, calling out apologies to all the people whose ribs I was accidentally elbowing or whose toes I was stepping on. The guy was big, and between his height and that neon green shirt it was easy to keep him in sight even over the heads of the people between us. But it wasn't easy to keep up with him, and by the time I reached the edge of the crowd, he was already halfway across the open area between the metal crowd barriers and the big speaker tower at the edge of the stage.

"Hey, stop!" I yelled. But Toni Lovely had just finished a song, and my voice was lost in the cheers all around me.

Mr. Scar clambered up the base of the speaker tower onto a wooden platform about five feet up. He paused just long enough to glance down at me, then disappeared behind one of the big pieces of electrical equipment on the platform.

My heart was pounding as I skidded to a stop at the base of the tower and looked up. The structure rose to a dizzying height above me, all metal fretwork and plywood platforms. It was like the Eiffel Tower of rock music, with enormous speakers on several levels and cords hanging here and there like festive streamers. From where I was standing it was impossible to see more than a level or two up, and I couldn't tell where the fake guard had gone. Was he directly above me in the fretwork somewhere? Or had he just used the speaker tower as a quick route backstage or elsewhere?

Only one way to find out, I decided. Grabbing hold of the metal support bars, I started climbing.

A couple of guys passing along the side of the stage saw me and shouted something. I ignored them, but realized I'd better keep toward the back of the tower to avoid being seen by the real guards out front. Somehow I didn't think they would approve.

The speakers were blasting Toni Lovely's latest song at what seemed like a million decibels, making it hard to think. I kept climbing, aiming for the area behind the first level of speakers. As I swung myself up like a little kid on the monkey bars, I found myself very glad that I was wearing shorts and sneakers rather than the sun-dress Bess had suggested.

It was a little quieter once I reached the area behind the speaker. I paused to catch my breath and look around, scanning the area above me for any sign of my quarry. The sides of the tower this high up were draped with a big banner with the Rockapazooma logo on it, which blocked out most of the sun and made it dim and hard to see much beyond the shadowy framework surrounding me.

I glanced down and out past the edge of the speaker, wondering if the fake guard had gone back down to try to blend in with the real guards. It was only then that I realized how high I'd already climbed. The view was dizzying and a little unnerving.

For the first time I paused long enough to think about the situation. *What in the world am I doing? This is crazy. I should forget about trying to catch up to that guy and go report him to security. I wonder if Deirdre even bothered to do that, or if she's just planning to report him to her best buddy Kijani instead?*

I bit my lip and looked around, clinging to one of the metal support beams as I tried to figure out the safest way down. Just then a few pebbles or something rained down on the plywood floor at my feet. I glanced up and spotted a flash of green somewhere overhead.

There he is! I thought with a fresh burst of adrenaline. *He's not that far ahead anymore.*

I scrambled up another few levels, straining my eyes as I peered into the dimness above. Soon I was just about even with the lights at the top of the stage. Another glance down revealed Toni Lovely blowing kisses to the crowd as she finished her final song. But I didn't have time to stop and watch. I'd just caught another spurt of movement above me.

It had come from directly over the stage this time. Climbing as quickly as I could, I moved hand-over-hand across a beam and then onto a slender metal cat-walk connecting two blocks of lighting. I knew that the stage was beneath me now, though I didn't dare look down again.

Okay, now where did he go? I wondered, my heart in my throat as I carefully knelt on the narrow walkway and then rose to a standing position, supporting myself against a phone-booth-sized black box that seemed to be part of the lighting paraphernalia. I made my way around it, my back pressed against its smooth surface.

I rounded the far side . . . and found myself face-to-face with Mr. Scar!

He was staring right at me, his face twisted in an angry scowl. "Who are you and what do you want?" he demanded. His voice was thick with a foreign accent I didn't recognize.

I froze, suddenly realizing how vulnerable I was, balanced on a narrow spit of metal grating some sixty feet above the stage. The fake guard must have realized it at the same moment. With a snarl, he lunged forward and gave me a hard shove.

"No!" I cried, feeling one foot slip off the catwalk into thin air. I scrabbled for a hold on the smooth boxy object behind me, but there was nothing to hold on to. I twisted around and managed to grab a nearby beam just in time to avoid losing my balance. In the process, my hand grazed the guard's face, knocking off his baseball cap. The hat tumbled away into the darkness, revealing the raised white scar snaking its way across the right side of his head.

The guy came at me again, but this time I was ready for him. I dodged to one side, easily avoiding his flying fist, and then skittered along the catwalk. Glancing back over my shoulder to see if he was gaining on me, I saw that he was clambering off down the rigging in the opposite direction.

He's getting away! I thought. If I could only keep him in sight until I managed to attract the attention of the real guards . . .

I turned around and went after him, moving as quickly as I could without risking a fall. By now I was breathing so hard from the exertion of the chase that I could barely hear anything else. Squinting in a vain attempt to spot where the guard was gone, I held my breath to listen for the sound of his shoes clanging against the metal beams as he climbed across the rigging.

Suddenly Mack-Daddy's distinctive voice blasted out of the speakers as he started to introduce the next act. It wasn't quite as loud up there in the rigging, since all the speakers were pointing out toward the audience, but it still drowned out everything else.

I paused, feeling helpless as I peered ahead into the shadowy reaches of the rigging. Where had the guy gone? Had he pulled too far ahead for me to catch him? Or had he, perhaps, doubled back and come around behind me, waiting for the chance to sneak up and make another attempt to push me to my doom?

At that moment the emcee paused briefly in his patter. In the brief seconds of relative quiet, I heard a sort of grunting sound just off to my right. Aha!

Moving as silently as I could, I headed in that direction. There was an enormous light fixture in my way. I carefully maneuvered myself over it to the other side—and froze.

Two teenage boys were crouched on a beam just a few feet away, staring back at me.

CHAPTER 9

JOE

CHASING ANSWERS

When the cute redhead appeared out of nowhere up in the rigging above the stage, I just about fell off the beam where Frank and I were standing. We'd been climbing around up there for a while, trying to find the spot with the best view of the concert grounds.

At least that's what *I* was doing. Frank was mostly trying to convince me we should climb back down. He's no fun at all.

But back to the girl. (Did I mention she was cute?)

She was staring at us as if we were ghosts or something. And no wonder. It was pretty weird to run into someone up there.

"Who are you?" she demanded.

"Who are *you*?" Frank shot back. That's my brother for you—he has a real way with words.

I decided to expand the line of questioning. "What are you doing up here?" I asked. "Are you part of the crew or something?"

"The crew?" She looked down. You could sort of see the stage through the spaces between these planks a few feet below where we were. The second band on the bill, these crazy Irish guys called the Bootstraps, had just come out. They were dancing around, waving their instruments at the audience.

Frank scooted a little closer to the girl and gave her a suspicious look. "So, are you—"

Before he could finish, a shout went up from somewhere nearby. "Hey! You there!"

Uh-oh.

I looked over and saw a pair of security guards in their bright green T-shirts climbing up the scaffolding toward us. One guy had shaggy blond hair and a big nose. The other was thin as a rail, but muscular and tough-looking.

Both of them looked mad.

"Friends of yours?" the girl asked us.

Frank shook his head grimly. "This way," he said. "Come on!"

The girl and I both followed as Frank scrambled off

across the rigging. I was right behind the girl, and the view was a little distracting.

So was the music. The Bootstraps had finally stopped jumping around. They tore into their first number, a recent hit song called "Watch Your Mouth."

"Whoa, I love this song!" I whispered to myself.

Just then, I heard another shout from one of the guards behind us. It sounded close.

Oops. Time to focus. We had to escape. If those guards were friends of our old buddy Tyreese, we would be in big trouble.

Scratch that. They'd just caught us climbing around in the rafters right above the stage. We were in big trouble either way.

Frank led us a little higher into the rigging, then headed across the stage toward the opposite side. Halfway across, the girl glanced down.

"Hey," I called to her breathlessly. "This is no time to stop and watch the show."

The girl shot me an annoyed look. "They're cutting us off!" she cried. "We have to go back the way we came."

I looked down. She was right. The blond guard had split off from the other guy and was now sneaking up toward us from another angle, trying to block our escape route.

The girl was already turning back. She grabbed a

pole and swung herself across a space between two planks.

"Come on, bro!" I called over my shoulder to Frank. "This way!"

The girl was a total maniac, swinging from beam to beam like some kind of demented Tarzanette.

Pretty cool.

I followed her. It wasn't easy keeping up. Behind me, I could hear the sound of Frank panting.

A little farther behind, the guards were shouting. They didn't sound happy.

"Faster," I cried, leaping down from a metal mesh platform onto a sheet of plywood four or five feet below.

"Careful!" The girl lowered herself partway down one of the support beams, then dropped lightly beside me. "Some of these things aren't that sturdy. It's safer to climb down than to jump."

"Whatever," I said. "Maybe I should just hang around and wait for those guards to escort me down. That sounds even safer."

She just rolled her eyes. "Come on," she said, grabbing a pole and sliding down another level.

I grinned and followed. Not only was she cute, she was bossy, too. I kind of liked that.

After that we didn't slow down until we were back on the ground and a good hundred yards from the stage. We finally stopped between the back of an ice cream stand and a row of Dumpsters. Aside from the smell of garbage, there was nothing to bother us back there. Even the music was muffled.

I leaned against the back wall of the ice cream stand, trying to catch my breath. Now that we were out in the sunshine, I could finally get a good look at the girl.

My first impression had been right; she was really easy on the eyes. Reddish-blond hair, pretty face. Not flashy or anything, but cute.

She also looked kind of familiar.

"Do I know you?" I asked, searching my mind to try to place where I'd seen her. Not to brag or anything, but I *do* meet a lot of girls. I just couldn't recall where I'd encountered this particular one. "I'm Joe, by the way. That's my brother, Frank."

"Shut up, *Jimmy,*" Frank whispered from between clenched teeth.

Oops. I'd forgotten for a second that we were supposed to be undercover. Maybe that was why he always says I get too distracted by girls.

Luckily the girl didn't seem to have noticed anything. I figured it was no big deal. At least I hadn't given away our last name.

"I'm Nancy." She smiled at both of us and stuck out her hand.

Frank just stared at it. He can be so dense.

"Hi there," I said with my most charming smile, grabbing her hand before Frank could get near it. "I'm Joe. Nice to meet you."

"Um, yeah," Frank said. "Now I'm afraid we have to be going. Enjoy the concert."

He grabbed me and dragged me off. We ducked through a crowd of dancing concert-goers. Then we made a few zigzags. I guess Frank wanted to make extra sure she couldn't follow us. Soon we were back behind the speaker tower.

"Hey," I protested. "You didn't have to be so rude."

"You already told her our real names," Frank said. "I wanted to get you out of there before you gave away anything else."

I rolled my eyes. "Give me some credit, man. I'm not completely stupid. Besides, what if she's part of that other ATAC team that's supposed to be here along with us?"

"ATAC? Wait, you guys work for ATAC? So it *is* real!"

I whirled around. Nancy was standing right there behind us. Her eyes were gleaming with interest.

"How did you do that?" I blurted. "How'd you follow us back here?"

She shrugged. "It's sort of what I do. Now about ATAC . . ."

"Joe!" Frank exclaimed, sounding pained.

I know, I know. Me and my big mouth.

"Um, did I say ATAC?" I said quickly. "I meant, uh . . .

"You meant ATAC. As in American Teens Against Crime."

She was staring at me as if I were a bug squirming at the end of a pin she'd just stuck in me. Only in this case, I guess you could say I'd stuck it in myself. How could I be so stupid? Not only had I totally forgotten about our fake names, but I'd just accidentally given away our biggest secret to a complete stranger.

"How do you know about ATAC?" Frank asked.

Nancy shrugged. "My friend George came across something about it on some blog just a couple of weeks ago. She knew I'd be interested, so she forwarded it to me." She laughed. "Of course, my friend Bess thinks it's all just some conspiracy theory, and that something like that couldn't possibly exist."

"Your friend Bess is right," Frank said. "It doesn't exist."

Nancy ignored him. "So you guys are both ATAC agents?" she asked eagerly. "How'd you get involved with the group? Are you on a mission right now? Is something going down at the concert?"

I was still struggling with the concept of a girl named George. But I pushed that aside.

"Listen, my brother's right," I said. "I was just kidding around. I read about ATAC on that blog too, and I was just joking around."

"Really?" Her eyes were like bright blue lasers boring into me. "Which blog was it?"

"Huh?"

"Which blog?" she repeated. "Where did you read about it?"

"It was . . . um . . ." A fly buzzed past in front of my face. I shooed it away, wishing I could buzz away with it. I stared up at the enormous speaker tower looming over us, hoping for inspiration. All I saw were a bunch of cables, wires, and knobs sticking out of the backs of the huge speakers.

Oh, and Frank's scowling face, of course. Not much help there.

A smile was spreading across Nancy's face. "That's what I thought," she said. "So how long have you guys been with the group? What kind of cases have you worked on? Are you on a case now? Does it have something to do with that guy I was chasing? You said you were *here* with ATAC, so I'm guessing that's a yes. . . ."

"That's none of your business." Frank's voice was harsh. "Now, I suggest you go away and forget you ever met us. And never tell a soul."

"Look, you can trust me," she said. "I'm sort of an amateur detective myself. If the stuff on that blog was right, I think what you guys do is totally cool."

"That's nice." Frank still sounded cold and angry.

Probably mostly at me. "Perhaps that blog also mentioned that ATAC is a *secret* agency."

"Yeah," I added. "Sorry."

Nancy looked annoyed. "Come *on,*" she said. "I just saved your butts up there. Don't I at least deserve a few answers?"

"*You* saved *our* butts?" I let out a laugh. "Get real. We saved you!"

"Oh, *please.*" She gave us a weary look, and leaned back against the edge of the stage. "I'm starting to think the reason you won't tell me anything is because you don't know anything. Maybe you did just read about ATAC on that blog, and now you're playing spy and pretending to be something you're not."

I exchanged a glance with Frank. What kind of jerks did she take us for? She was totally working us—trying to insult us so we'd slip up and tell her what she wanted to know.

It was almost impressive. Who *was* this girl?

"You guys still haven't figured out why I look familiar, have you?" she added.

"I never said I thought you looked familiar," Frank said. "That's just one of Joe's pickup lines."

"No, it wasn't," Nancy said. "I recognized you guys as soon as I saw you out in the light too. Only *I* remembered where I'd seen you right away."

Okay, so the smug look wasn't so cute on her. I frowned. "Are you going to tell us, or what?"

"It was an hour or two ago." She stared at me with those laser-beam blue eyes again. "Joe, you came running up and tried to flirt with my friend Bess. Then Frank came and dragged you away."

"Whoa." I suddenly flashed back to the encounter. She was right—that was totally where I'd seen her before. The problem was, I'd been so focused on the blonde that I'd barely registered Nancy's face at the time. "*That's* your friend Bess?"

Frank just looked annoyed. "Okay, whatever," he said. "The point is, you really need to forget we ever mentioned ATAC. Just go enjoy the show, and forget we ever—"

I was still staring at her, so I saw her eyes suddenly widen. She leaped toward us.

"Look out!" she yelled, giving Frank a hard shove on the chest.

"Oof!" He stumbled back.

"Hey!" I cried at the same time. "What are you—"

Crash!

One of the huge speakers from the tower overhead smashed into the ground . . . exactly where Frank had just been standing.

CHAPTER 10

NANCY

COMPARING NOTES

Speaker parts went flying everywhere. The two guys were shouting, sounding startled.

I jumped back and stared up at the tower. That couldn't have been an accident. . . .

Sure enough, I spotted a flash of green. It was that guard! He peered down for a second, then turned away.

"It's him!" I cried, pointing. "It's the guy I was chasing!"

Mr. Green Shirt scrambled across the tower and jumped down on the far side. I took off after him, rounding the corner of the stage. Spying a flash of green heading back toward the refreshment stands, I ran that way. When I skidded around the edge of a pizza tent, tons of people were waiting in line or clustered around the condiment table. I got there just in time to see the fake guard dodge around a baby stroller and sprint off into the crowd.

"Nancy, wait!" one of the guys called behind me. I think it was Joe. He seemed to be the more talkative of the pair.

Ignoring him, I ran off in hot pursuit. But I had to stop when a two-year-old boy wandered into my path and almost dropped his hot dog on my foot. Who brings a toddler to a rock concert, anyway?

Dodging the kid, I paused to look around for Mr. Scar. That's when I felt someone grab me.

Spinning around, I saw that it was Frank. He was staring at me with a look of confusion in his deep brown eyes.

"Who *are* you?" he asked.

Twisting my arm, I yanked free of his grip. But when I looked around, there was no sign of the guard. I sighed and went limp. There was no way I was going to catch up with him in this crowd.

The two guys dragged me off behind another food stand. This one sold hot dogs and hamburgers, and the little alleyway behind it stank of onions and pickle juice.

This time they were the ones with questions. "What's going on here?" Frank demanded.

"Yeah," Joe added. "You look like a regular girl, but you sure don't act like one!"

I was still annoyed that they wouldn't tell me anything about ATAC. The mysterious crime-fighting group had been in the back of the mind ever since George had showed me that site.

At first glance I'd been inclined to agree with Bess—ATAC looked more like the brainchild of some movie producer or comic book writer than a real-life group. But the blogger, who was some kind of true-crime junkie, seemed convinced. By the time I'd finished reading, so was I. At least mostly. If ATAC didn't really exist, I figured it *should*.

I'd asked George to do a little more research online. She's much better than I am at that stuff. Unfortunately, she hadn't turned up much. A few references, a little speculation, and not much in the way of facts.

Next I'd gone to my dad. He has lots of friends in the government, and I figured he could call in some favors. He'd promised to ask around, but he didn't seem very interested. And soon after that I sort of forgot the whole thing myself for a while due to another mystery popping up.

And now here were these guys. Somehow I'd been imagining that ATAC agents would be . . . different, I guess. Suave and sophisticated, maybe. Or gruff and tough. But Frank and Joe were just ordinary teenage guys.

Still, a mystery was a mystery. If these guys really were ATAC agents, I needed to share what I knew. It seemed kind of unlikely that some guy grabbing Deirdre Shannon could be connected to an official ATAC case, but you never know.

"You're not the only ones who spend a lot of time solving crimes," I told them.

"We never admitted we—" Frank began quickly.

But Joe gave him a shove on the arm. "Quiet, Frank," he said. "Let her talk." He stared at me. "What do you mean?"

"My name is Nancy Drew, and I—"

"Nancy *Drew*?" Frank's eyes widened. "Whoa! Are you serious?"

Joe glanced over at him. "You've heard of her?"

"We both have, Joe," Frank said. "Don't you remember? Dad showed us an article about her from that Midwestern newspaper a month or so ago. She's the one who cracked that big fraud case that happened out here. The article said she's solved all kinds of other big mysteries too."

"Oh, yeah!" Joe's expression cleared. "I forgot the name, but now that you mention it . . . Dad was totally impressed. He said she'd probably make a heck of an ATAC agent."

"Really?" I couldn't help being flattered by that.

Then I thought back over what they'd just said, and something else clicked into place in my mind. "Wait—your last name isn't Hardy, is it?"

"How did you know that?" Frank immediately looked suspicious again. He seemed to look that way a lot.

"ATAC is a secret group, right?" I shrugged. "So if your dad knows about it, I'm guessing your dad is Fenton Hardy, the retired New York City detective and successful private investigator who helped found ATAC." I smiled sweetly, enjoying the looks of consternation on their faces. "At least that's what it said on that blog. If I recall correctly."

Joe sighed. "You recall correctly," he admitted. "That's Dad."

"Joe!" Frank looked as if his head was about to explode. He definitely seemed like the more tightly wound of the two.

"Give it up, Frank. She's totally onto us," Joe said. From what I could tell so far, he was the *opposite* of tightly wound. "Anyway, maybe this is a good thing. Maybe she can help us figure out what we're supposed to be doing here."

"No way." Frank glared at his brother furiously. "You blabbing our biggest secrets to some random girl is definitely *not* a good thing."

"Relax," I said, brushing off Frank's comment. "I'm

practically a professional too. You know that. I can keep a secret. Maybe I can even help, like Joe said."

"You are *not* a professional," Frank said. "You may have solved a few local burglaries or whatever, but that doesn't mean you're ready to jump in and help us."

I rolled my eyes. "Whatever," I said. "I guess you're lucky that little amateur me was there to save your necks just now." I nodded in the direction of the speaker tower. "*Again,*" I added, thinking back to our first close call up in the same tower.

"Right." Joe cleared his throat. "I'm sure Frank does appreciate that. Right, Frank?"

"Sure," Frank said grudgingly. "Thanks."

"You're welcome." I turned to Joe. "Wait a second. Did you just say something about not knowing what you're doing here? Are you on a case right now or not?"

Joe shot his brother an uncertain glance. "Um . . . "

Frank sighed loudly. "You don't miss much, do you, Nancy Drew?" he said. "Fine. If we tell you what we know, do you swear you won't tell anyone?"

I crossed my heart with one finger. "I'm listening."

"We're here on a mission," Frank said. "There's just one problem: We don't know what it is, exactly."

"Huh?"

"ATAC told us to come here and keep our eyes open," Joe said. "They said something might go down at the show. But that's all we know. They're not usually that vague; I'm not sure what to make of it."

For a moment, I wondered if they were still keeping secrets from me. But I'm pretty good at reading people. And both guys looked sincere. Well, Joe looked sincere. Frank still looked annoyed and kind of uncertain. So I figured they were probably telling the truth.

"Weird," I said. "So did you spot that fake guard too? Is that why you were up in the scaffolding?"

"Fake guard?" Joe repeated. "What fake guard?"

"Wait." Now I was getting confused. "If you weren't chasing him, why'd he try to kill you just now with that speaker? I got a look at him just after he managed to get it pushed over, and it was definitely the same guy I was chasing up in the scaffolding."

"Really?" Joe glanced over toward the speaker tower, as if expecting Mr. Scar to be standing up there waving at us.

"Hmm. Guess he was trying to kill *me*," I said. "His aim's not too good."

Frank was starting to look kind of irritated again. "Look, maybe you'd better start from the beginning," he told me.

"Good idea." I took a deep breath of the grease-scented air. "See, there's this girl I know named Deirdre. . . ."

I quickly outlined the events of the day so far, trying not to leave out anything that might be important.

First I described Deirdre herself, including her family's wealth. Then I told them how we'd come upon her haranguing the security guard outside the backstage gate, and soon afterward, witnessed the man dragging her away.

". . . so we ran over to see what was going on," I continued. "When we confronted the guy, he didn't say anything—just dropped Deirdre and took off in the other direction. I suspected he wasn't a real guard once I realized he was the only one not wearing a name tag."

"Good observation," Frank said. "Did you get a good look at him?"

I nodded. "He was tall and big, like most of the guards." I closed my eyes for a moment, calling up a mental picture. "Dark skin, shaved head, and a big, ugly scar running up and over the left side of his head."

"And that's who you were chasing up there?" Joe glanced in the direction of the stage.

"Uh-huh. I spotted him again later and followed him up the tower." The guard's scowling face flashed into my mind, along with the panic I'd felt when I'd realized how easy it would be for him to push me off the scaffolding. "He spoke to me that time—he had a foreign accent. Oh, and he was wearing a DJ Razz cap. Do you think that means—" I cut myself off with a gasp. "Hey!" I exclaimed. "It wasn't the same guy!"

"What?" Frank sounded confused.

I was scanning the images in my head. The guy who'd grabbed Deirdre . . . . the guy up in the tower . . .

"The scars," I said, wondering how I'd missed it earlier. "They both had them. But the first guy's scar was on the left side of his skull, and the other guy's was on the right."

"Hold on." Joe raised one hand. "You're saying you've been chasing *two* big guard-looking dudes with scars on their heads? And you just figured out they were two different guys?"

"Their faces are almost identical," I said. "They must be brothers at least, if not twins."

I saw the Hardys exchange a dubious look. "Are you yanking our chain?" Joe asked. "If this is some weird way to try and find out more about ATAC . . ."

"This isn't about stupid ATAC!" I was getting fed up with their attitude. "I'm telling you, there are two look-alike guys running around attacking people at this concert. And since you two don't even know what your own ATAC mission is about, I don't think you should be—"

"Aha!" George's voice crowed from just behind me. "So this is where you sneaked off to, Nancy."

Spinning around, I gulped. Bess and George were standing at the corner of the hot dog stand, peering back at us. They were both holding sodas, and George had a container of fries, too.

"We thought we heard you while we were in line out front," Bess said. "Were you ever planning to come back out to watch the show?"

George nodded, glancing curiously from me to the Hardys and back again. "Yeah," she said. "And what's all this about ATAC?"

CHAPTER 11

FRANK

JUST TUNED IN . . .

I groaned, my heart sinking into my Nikes. It was bad enough we'd accidentally revealed ourselves to one outsider. Now there were *three*?

For a second I dared to hope that Nancy's friends hadn't heard much. But I guess that was too much to ask.

"Are you talking about that teen superspy group thingy you found on the Internet?" the blond girl asked.

"That's the one." The dark-haired girl glanced at me with a sharp expression. "ATAC—American Teens something-something."

"Against Crime," Joe said helpfully.

"Shut up!" I hissed at him through clenched teeth.

Meanwhile Nancy looked kind of sheepish. I guess she was as surprised by her friends' arrival as we were.

"Guys, these are my best friends Bess Marvin and George Fayne." She pointed to the pretty blonde and the dark-haired girl in turn. "And these guys are Frank and Joe Hardy."

My mind was working at warp speed. This was a disaster. We had to figure out a plan to ditch these girls fast.

I glanced at Joe. But he wasn't looking in my direction. He was staring at Nancy's friend Bess. And he didn't look upset at all.

"Nice to meet you ladies," he said.

He was using what he thinks is his supersuave Mr. Charming voice. In reality it makes him sound like a total tool.

"Hey, aren't you that dork who was flirting with Bess earlier?" George asked Joe.

He looked so annoyed that I almost cracked a smile. Almost.

"We did almost meet earlier," he said. "I remember it well. You girls really stand out in a crowd."

"That's nice." Bess turned to Nancy. "So where'd you run off to, anyway?"

"Remember that guy who grabbed Deirdre? I spotted him again," Nancy replied. "Except it wasn't actually him—it was someone who looked almost exactly like him."

George let out a groan. "I should have known you'd turn that Deirdre thing into a full-fledged mystery! So are these two with ATAC? Did you recruit them to help you track down the bad guys?"

"Not exactly." Nancy hesitated and glanced at Joe and me. "Can I tell them?"

Joe didn't answer. He was still staring at Bess. I was amazed he wasn't actually drooling.

"Go ahead," I said, too exasperated with the whole situation to argue about it anymore. "You might as well tell them the whole freaking story. In fact, why don't you call over one of those roving TV camera crews? That way we can put it up on the big screens so everyone at the concert knows all our secrets too."

"Chill, Frank," Joe said. "It's not that big a deal."

How could he be so calm? Usually *he* was the hyper one! And this was only our entire ATAC career at stake.

"Right. Five heads are better than three, right?" Nancy added.

I took a few deep breaths and thought about that. She had a point. It wasn't as if Joe and I were making much headway on the mission so far. I mean, we didn't even know what our mission *was*.

Maybe we should think of these girls as bystanders we're interviewing, I told myself. *Okay, so maybe we don't usually let bystanders in on the whole ATAC thing. But what's that thing Aunt Trudy always says about crying over spilled milk?*

I took a few more deep breaths. We might as well roll with it.

At least for now.

"Fine," I said. "Go ahead, Nancy. Fill them in."

"Thanks." Nancy turned to her friends. "So Frank and Joe work for ATAC, and their latest mission was to come here to the concert. . . ."

Soon Bess and George were up to speed. To my surprise, they didn't seem that shocked or scared.

"So what do we know so far?" Bess tapped her chin with one finger. It was a little distracting. She was really cute. "There's a pair of matching thugs with big scars and foreign accents running around this place. One of them tried to grab Deirdre, and another just tried to kill Nancy—or possibly you guys."

George glanced at me. "Does that sound like it could be part of your mission?"

"Maybe." I still wasn't totally comfortable with this group discussion thing. But my mind was clicking back into gear. "Hey, Nancy, didn't you say the guy you chased was wearing a DJ Razz cap?"

"Yeah," she said. "I almost forgot about that. Do you think this could have something to do with Razz?"

"Could be," George said. "I heard Razz once went to jail for punching a cop. And a couple of his bodyguards got arrested a couple of months ago up in Chicago for, like, aggravated assault or something. I think they beat up another rapper's assistant."

Bess wrinkled her nose. "Lovely."

"Maybe we should check it out." Joe glanced at me. "Feel like sneaking backstage again, Frank?"

"You know it." I patted my jeans pocket, checking for my mini-cattle-prod. Just in case. "You girls wait here. We'll let you know what we find."

"I don't think so!" Nancy exclaimed. "If you're sneaking backstage, we're coming with you."

I was a little annoyed. Just because we'd let them in on some of the details of our mission didn't make them full-fledged agents.

But I also couldn't help a flash of admiration. She definitely wasn't like any girl I'd ever met before.

"Fine," I said. "Then come on, let's go."

We headed off through the crowd. The stage was empty at the moment except for some workers rushing around setting things up for the next band. Up on the big screens, Annie Wu was interviewing some concert-goers about their thoughts on global warming.

Soon we were approaching our secret spot in the fence. "Keep quiet," Joe whispered. "Just slide through here, one at a—"

"Hey! I thought I told you boys I didn't want to see you around here again!"

I groaned. What were the odds?

Sure enough, when I turned around, our pal Tyreese was lumbering toward us. He looked even more enormous than I remembered. Angrier, too.

"You know this guy?" George muttered to me.

"Sort of. He kicked us out of the backstage area earlier."

Tyreese had reached us by now. He grabbed Joe by the arm. "You boys must be slow learners," he rumbled.

"Excuse me," Bess said sweetly. She stepped forward. "I'm sure there's been some kind of misunderstanding. . . ."

Tyreese dropped Joe's arm. "Oh, sorry, Ms. Lovely. I didn't see you there."

For a second I thought the guard was just overwhelmed by Bess's beauty. Then I realized he wasn't just referring to her as lovely. He'd mistaken her for Toni Lovely, the singer!

"Um . . . that's okay," Bess said, playing along. "I—I forgot my backstage pass, so my friends and I were just going to slip through here so as not to bother anyone."

Tyreese let out something that sounded like an elephant choking up a hairball. I think it was a chuckle.

"No sweat, Ms. Lovely." He shot me and Joe a slightly suspicious glance. "I didn't realize these young men were with you."

"No harm done." Bess patted him on the arm and

smiled. She peered up at his name tag. "Thanks for doing such a good job, Tyreese!"

We scurried through the fence opening. I didn't dare look back at the guard. What if he caught on to us?

But soon we were inside. When I glanced over my shoulder, Tyreese had already turned away.

"Wow," George exclaimed as we all hurried out of sight around the nearest trailer. "I can't believe that worked!"

"Yeah," Joe said. "You're way better looking than Toni Lovely, Bess."

"Never mind that." Nancy was looking around with interest. "You guys have been back here before, right? Do you know where DJ Razz's trailer is?"

Joe shook his head. "We can show you Lethal Injection's, though. Right, Frank?"

"Are you an LI fan?" George asked Joe, her face lighting up. "They're awesome, aren't they? I hope we get this mystery wrapped up in time to go back out and watch their set. I can't wait to see what the death scene is today!"

"I can." Joe sounded smug. "Frank and I already know what it's going to be."

"No way!" George punched Joe in the arm. "Are you serious? What is it? How did you find out?"

Joe pretended to zip his lip. "Sorry, can't tell."

"Hey, there's Ned!" Nancy broke in. She waved at someone farther down the row of trailers.

I had no idea who Ned was. Turning to look, I saw a tall guy walking toward us. Right at his elbow was a pretty dark-haired girl dressed in a low-cut top.

George was looking at them too. "Great. Looks like Deirdre finally whined her way backstage."

"Deirdre?" I said. "That's the girl you mentioned before, right? The one who got grabbed by the first fake guard."

"Yeah, that's her," Nancy replied. "And the guy with her is my boyfriend, Ned Nickerson."

It figured. The smart, good-looking ones always have boyfriends. This Ned guy looked like the type girls always go for, too—tall, brown hair, broad-shoulders. He could've stepped right out of Hollywood.

Joe leaned toward me. "Check out Captain America," he whispered, rolling his eyes.

Soon we were all trading introductions. Ned turned out to have a firm, hearty handshake. Big surprise there.

"Nice to meet you guys," he said. "Are you friends of Nancy's?"

"Um, sort of," I said.

Luckily he was already turning away to shake hands with Joe, so I didn't have to come up with a cover story. Meanwhile the girl, Deirdre, was coming toward me.

"Hi there," she said. "It's nice to meet you, Frank."

She seemed friendly. *Very* friendly. Especially when she took my hand in both of hers, stepping so close I could smell her minty-fresh breath. Usually I get flustered when stuff like that happens, but this time I just felt a little weirded out. "So where are you boys from?" Deirdre asked.

"Back east," I said.

Nearby, Joe was staring at me through narrowed eyes. He always gets all weird when girls pay more attention to me than to him. When I shifted my gaze to avoid his stare, I noticed that Nancy was whispering something in Ned's ear. Was she telling him about ATAC?

"Ooo, do you live anywhere near New York City?" Deirdre exclaimed. She dropped my hand. But before I could step back to a more comfortable conversational distance, she grabbed my upper arm and squeezed it. "Oh my gosh, I love it there! The shopping, the fashion, the stores . . ."

"That's our DeeDee," George said. "All about the culture."

"Shut up, *Georgia,*" Deirdre snapped back without taking her eyes off my face. "Nobody's talking to you. As usual."

Ah—Georgia. At least now George's name made sense. But I didn't think about that for long. I was feeling more awkward with every passing second. Every passing second in which Deirdre continued to snuggle up against me, that is.

"Uh, we don't live in New York City," I told her. "We're from a town called Bayport."

"Oh." Deirdre shrugged. "That sounds nice too. You'll have to tell me all about it."

Still clinging to my arm, she sort of pressed up against me. I wasn't sure what to do. Joe may be Mr. Cool with girls, but I'm not. I can't even fake it that well. Call me a dork—Joe always does.

"Excuse me," I blurted. "I—I—Nancy, can I talk to you about something?"

Okay, so Nancy's a girl too. But she was the first name that popped out. Besides, she's a different kind of girl. Not like Deirdre.

"Sure, Frank." Nancy followed as I pulled free of Deirdre and hurried off a short distance. "What is it?"

"Um . . ." I searched for an excuse, but I drew a blank. My face started to go red.

Nancy glanced back at the group. They were all standing around where we'd left them, chatting. Deirdre was laughing at something Joe had just said.

"Oh," Nancy said. "Just needed some space from Deirdre, huh? I understand. She can be a little pushy."

Man, she was perceptive. I wasn't sure whether to be embarrassed or relieved. I settled for a shrug.

"Whatever," I muttered. "But look, we should keep

moving on this DJ Razz thing. He'll be performing before too long, and then who knows if he'll stick around."

"You're right. Plus we might get kicked out of here any second." Nancy glanced back at the others. "Maybe you and I should go try to sneak in right now. We can't go over there with this huge group."

I knew Joe would be less than thrilled with the plan, but I nodded. It looked like he had his hands full—he was standing right between Bess and Deirdre. It was like his dream come true.

"Should we let them know we're going?" I asked.

"I'll tell George." Nancy dashed back and whispered something to her friend. A moment later she was back. "Let's go."

We slipped around the corner, out of sight. It didn't take long to find Razz's trailer. We figured it had to be the one with the huge airbrushed portrait of him on the side.

There was also a tough-looking dude standing outside the door. He glared at everyone who walked past.

"Bodyguard," I murmured into Nancy's ear. "We'll have to look for another way in."

We snuck around the corner of the trailer when the bodyguard wasn't looking. There was a sort of alleyway back there, formed by two rows of trailers and buses backing up to a line of utility outlets. We soon found Razz's back door.

Nancy slipped up the metal steps without a sound and tried the handle. "Locked," she whispered.

"Let me up there." We traded places, and I pulled out my wallet. Within seconds I'd picked the lock with the tiny plastic gadget I keep in there for times like these.

"Impressive," she whispered as I eased open the door.

"All part of the job."

We peered inside. The back door opened into some kind of storage room. The lights were off, but the windows admitted enough light to see stacks of boxes and racks of clothes.

Muffled voices were coming from beyond another closed door. Nancy and I crept inside.

I couldn't quite make out what the voices were saying. It sounded like there were at least three people out there. One sounded like Razz himself. Another spoke too softly to hear much. And a third had a strong Spanish accent.

Now we're getting somewhere, I thought. *Nancy said that second guard had a foreign accent!*

We moved closer to the door, neither of us making a sound. I even held my breath. Maybe if we got close enough, we could hear what they were saying.

Just then there was a click from somewhere behind us. I froze. Before I could move, I heard heavy footsteps moving toward us. A second later a strong hand clamped down on my shoulder.

"Hey!" a voice said. "What are you two doing in here?"

CHAPTER 12

NANCY

BUSTED!

I felt a hand latch on to my shoulder. Beside me Frank let out a grunt of surprise.

Glancing up I saw a heavyset man towering over me. It didn't take a detective to figure out that he was probably one of DJ Razz's bodyguards.

"Oops," I said. "Um, I think we're in the wrong trailer. . . ."

"Nice try," the bodyguard said. "Come on, let's see what the boss wants me to do with you."

Frank shot me a helpless look. I knew how he felt. The bodyguard was huge and, judging by his grip on my shoulder, extremely strong. Even if one of us could twist away, there was no way we were both going to escape.

We were totally busted.

The guy dragged us over to the door and kicked at it. It swung open to reveal a larger, brightly lit room beyond. Five or six people turned to stare at us as he dragged us in.

"Check it out, boss," our captor said. "Just found these two sneaking around in the back room."

"Nice work, Clarence," said a man sitting in a swiveling chair. It took me a second to recognize him as DJ Razz. He had a blue shower cap on his head and a big white bib-type cloth around his neck. A woman was dabbing something on his cheeks. "Bring 'em closer."

The bodyguard shoved us in Razz's direction. The other people in the trailer were staring at us. I glanced around for any sign of the scar twins, but didn't see them.

"What were you doing back there?" Razz demanded.

Frank cleared his throat. "We're really sorry, sir," he said. "We, um . . . we're just fans."

"Hmm." Razz looked us up and down. "I should let my man Clarence take you back there and teach you a lesson about sneaking around where you don't belong. . . ." He paused, then grinned. "But I won't. Man, you should see your faces—you look so freaked out!"

The people watching burst out laughing. Even Clarence cracked a smile.

Razz swiveled around and grabbed a water bottle from the counter behind him. He took a long drink. "Look, if you want my siggie, just ask, all right? No need for breaking and entering, know what I'm saying?"

"Sure." Frank sounded relieved. "Thanks."

My mind was already returning to the case. Maybe it wasn't exactly how we'd planned it, but we were in. I definitely didn't want to waste the opportunity to find out the information we'd come for.

"I think we were talking to one of your guys outside," I said. "Um, big guy with a scar on his head? Green shirt?"

I glanced around, searching the faces for any glimmer of recognition. But everyone there just shrugged or looked confused.

"Scar on his head?" Razz shot the big bodyguard a look. "That one of our guys?"

"Don't think so, boss," Clarence said. "Johnson has a scar on his chin, though."

"Must have been another wannabe." Razz chuckled and set down his water bottle. "Okay," he said. "What do you want me to sign? Your shirts? Maybe an arm? That one only applies to the pretty lady." He winked at me.

Somehow I stopped my eyes from rolling. "Um, how about our ticket stubs?" I suggested, fishing into my pocket for mine.

"Good enough," Razz said. Frank and I handed over

our stubs and he signed them with a flourish. "There you go, kids. Hold it a sec—got one more thing for you, long as you're here." He reached into a big cardboard box and pulled out a baseball cap with his name on it. "Take a hat. We got plenty of 'em."

He tossed one to each of us. I looked at mine. It was identical to the one Scar Guy #2 had been wearing. "Thanks," I said.

Frank put on his hat. He looked pretty goofy in it. With his conservative haircut and neat polo shirt, he wasn't exactly the hip-hop type.

"Sorry to have bothered you," he told Razz. "We'll get out of your way now."

"Enjoy the show." Razz was already turning back toward the makeup artist, but Clarence and the others watched us as we headed for the front door.

We scurried past the guard outside, who glared at us in surprise. Soon we were jogging around the corner in search of our friends. A new band, the Rotten Punks, had taken over from the last act while we were inside. We could hear the fast beat of one of their songs thumping out of the speakers out front.

"Well, that was pretty awkward." Frank reached up to remove the Razz cap.

"Yeah. But did you see them when I asked about the scar guy? It didn't look like they knew what I was talking about."

He nodded. "I noticed that too. Nice work slipping that in, by the way."

"Thanks."

We found Ned, Bess, George, and Joe right where we'd left them. "Where's Deirdre?" I asked.

"She ran off when she heard Kijani was getting interviewed over at the press tent." George sounded disgusted, which she often does while talking about Deirdre. "I still can't believe she talked her way back here. It sounds like she's been making a real pest of herself."

"Never mind. Before she gets back, guess where we just were?" I quickly filled in the others on everything that had just happened.

"Dude!" Joe punched Frank on the arm. "I can't believe you got Razz's autograph. Did you get one for me?"

Frank tossed him the baseball cap. "Sorry. But you can have this."

"Sweet!" Joe pulled on the hat. "I saw a bunch of guys walking by with these after you two ran off. I think they're giving them out somewhere near here."

That was no surprise, judging by the big box of hats we'd seen in Razz's trailer. Now that I looked around, I did notice quite a few people with identical caps. I glanced down at the one in my hand. "I guess maybe the Razz hat wasn't much of a clue after all."

"Guess not." Ned smiled and squeezed my shoulder. "But it was a good thought. Do you have any other theories?"

"Not really." I sighed. "Looks like we're back at square one."

Bess shook her head. "I still can't imagine why someone would try to grab Deirdre at a concert like this," she said. "If you were trying to kidnap someone, why do it in the most public setting possible?"

"Well, she *has* been making a pest of herself," George pointed out. "Are we sure it wasn't just a security guard getting a little too fed up with her?" She shrugged. "I certainly couldn't blame him. I've wanted to strangle her myself at least a million times."

She had a point. But I couldn't quite believe that was all there was to this. "Okay, but why would the guy who grabbed her be the only one without a name tag?" I asked. "And why would he try to kill me by pushing over that speaker? It just doesn't make sense."

We must be missing something, I thought. *Some missing link, some vital clue . . .*

I glanced at the Hardy brothers to see if they had any ideas. They were standing close together, and Frank was whispering something to Joe.

Were they holding out on me? It was pretty obvious they weren't thrilled to have my friends and me in on their ATAC secrets, especially Frank. And now that I thought about it, it seemed a little suspicious that they didn't even know what their mission was about.

I can't solve this if I don't have all the information, I thought. *I need to figure out if they're really telling me everything they know about this case.*

George, Bess, and Ned were busy speculating about what Deirdre might be doing over at the press tent at that moment. But I wasn't really listening. I studied the Hardys out of the corner of my eye, trying to decide what to do.

One thing was clear. I had a better chance of finding out what I needed to know if I could get one of them off alone. But which one?

Joe, I decided almost immediately. *He's definitely the more talkative of the two. And Frank seems way too smart and serious to slip up and tell me something he doesn't want me to know.*

Now all I needed was an excuse.

I stepped over to the Hardys. "Hey, did you say you saw someone around here giving out those Razz caps?" I asked Joe. "Maybe we should go check it out. The guy giving out the caps might remember the scar guy—maybe even know who he is."

Frank looked doubtful. "Seems like a long shot."

"I know. But we might as well cover all the bases while we're here," I said.

"Good point," Joe said. "Besides, anything's better

than just standing around here. We'll be right back, Frank. Let's go, Nancy."

Joe and I hurried off down the trailer aisle. I found my pace automatically matching the beat of the song the band was playing out on stage. "So where's this guy with the hats?" I asked.

"I didn't see him myself," Joe replied. "But most of the people with the caps were coming from this direction." He pointed to a pair of pretty young women wearing Razz caps. "Like them, see?"

"Good enough." I didn't really care if we ever found the hat guy. I just needed a little time with Joe. "I'm sure we can find him."

We rounded the corner and entered the next row of trailers and buses. "Check it out," Joe said. "You'll never guess which band owns that boring-looking trailer up there." He pointed to a nondescript double-wide.

"Who?"

"Lethal Injection." Joe grinned. "Frank and I were in there earlier. That's how we found out about today's death scene."

It was obvious that he was dying to have me ask more about that. I didn't really care what Lethal Injection had planned for that day's set, but I decided it was as good a conversation starter as any.

"Cool," I said. "Sure you can't share the secret with me?"

"Sorry. Nick Needles and Mike Manslaughter swore us to secrecy."

"Oh well." I shrugged. "I guess working for ATAC gives you guys lots of practice keeping secrets, huh?"

"Totally. Just part of the job."

I let a few seconds pass in silence, not wanting to give myself away by seeming too eager. "Must be hard sometimes," I said as we continued down the aisle. "Especially keeping stuff from your friends. Do your cases make you miss school a lot?"

"Sometimes. That's one of the perks."

I chuckled. "Just *one* of the perks, huh?" I said. "So that means there are others?"

I held my breath, hoping this would work. If I played my cards right, I might not only get more information about this case—I might find out more about ATAC, too.

CHAPTER 13

JOE

CENTER STAGE

Okay, so Nancy was cute. But not so cute that I couldn't figure out what she was up to.

"Sure, tons of perks," I said with a straight face. "Tricked-out motorcycles. Lots of cool travel. And we both have the White House on speed dial." I clapped one hand over my mouth. "Whoops! Now that I've told you that, I'm afraid I'll have to kill you."

Nancy looked startled for a second, then frowned. "Very funny," she said. "I guess that means you don't want to answer the question."

"More like I don't want to be interrogated by Nancy Drew, girl detective." I stopped and turned to face her. "I mean, come on, who do you think you're dealing with here?"

She shrugged, her expression wavering between annoyed and sheepish. Finally she sighed.

"Fine, you caught me," she said. "But if you guys weren't so secretive about all this ATAC stuff . . ."

"We have to be," I said. "Think about it. If we went around blurting out how we're secret agents, how useful would we be to ATAC?"

"That didn't stop you from blurting it to me," Nancy said.

She *would* have to bring that up. "That was an unusual case," I told her. "You totally perplexed me with your beauty and razor-sharp wit."

That shut her up for a second. But only for a second.

"So you admit you're still keeping information from me?" she asked. "I mean, come on—you really expect me to believe you guys don't know what your mission here is about?"

"Hey, we thought it was weird too." I shrugged. "Usually ATAC's a little more detailed. So yeah, you know as much as we do."

She narrowed her eyes and studied my face. "Are you sure you're telling me everything?"

I raised one hand and crossed my heart. "Now do you believe me?"

"Unfortunately, I guess I do." She bit her lip. "I was sort of hoping you were keeping back some huge clue or something."

"I hear you. This case doesn't make much sense."

We started walking again. I hummed along with the Rotten Punks, who were playing one of their best songs. Too bad I wasn't getting to watch them. Still, hanging out with Nancy wasn't too bad a trade-off.

"So far our only real lead is those scar guys," she said.

"So you really think there are two of them?" I asked.

"I know there are. I definitely noticed the scars."

She did seem like a girl who noticed stuff. "Okay," I said. "So what could they want with your friend Deirdre? Has she ever been mixed up in anything shady?"

"She's not really the shady type. Talk about blurting stuff out—I don't think there's a pause button between her brain and her mouth, if you know what I mean."

Out onstage the Rotten Punks had just finished their song. *"Good-bye, Rockapazooma!"* the singer shouted into the microphone.

The concert was more than half over. We didn't have long to figure this out.

"So what are the possibilities?" I said. "What kind of crime could ATAC think might go down at a show like this?"

Nancy stopped and turned to face me again. "Drugs?" she said. "Maybe music piracy?"

Frank and I had come up with both theories about

thirty seconds after getting the mission CD. Still, I was kind of impressed. This girl was sharp.

"Whatever it is, we need to figure it out, like, five minutes ago," I said. "We need a plan."

"Maybe we should split up," she said. "Some of us can stay out front in the crowd, and the rest can try to sneak backstage—as in *really* backstage, not just back here." She glanced around at the trailers. "Those scar guys always seem to be somewhere near the stage. Maybe this way we'll be able to spot them and figure out what they're up to."

"Sounds good to me. Let's go talk to Frank."

As soon as we turned around, I spotted Frank and the others. They must've wandered after Nancy and me, because they were standing at the end of the row we were in.

When we got closer, I saw that Deirdre was pressed up against my brother. Nearby, Bess was glaring at her.

Typical. The girls always seem to go for that dorky-nice-guy thing Frank has going.

For once, though, I couldn't get too worked up about it. Bess and Deirdre were both hot, no doubt about that. But then there was Nancy. There was something different about her. I'd never met a girl like her.

"Yeeeaaarrrrrrgh!"

Suddenly there was an explosion of screams from

somewhere close by. Spinning around, I saw a bunch of people burst out of a trailer.

"Hey!" George cried. "It's Lethal Injection!"

She was right. The four band members were in full makeup and costume now. Mike Manslaughter had acid yellow makeup smeared over his face, and his wild purple wig stuck straight up from his head. Nick Needles looked taller than ever in neck to toe black leather, with his day-glo orange face and shaggy black hair floating above it like some kind of freaky sun.

The band members leaped and spun and pumped their fists in the air. A few bodyguards and other random people tagged along as they rushed up the aisle toward us.

"Whoo!" Mike Manslaughter yelled. "LI rules! We are the kings of darkness!"

I grinned. This was more like it! I remembered why I'd been so psyched to come to Rockapazooma.

"Whoo!" I yelled back.

"Hey!" Frank said. He yanked me behind Ned. "Don't let them see us."

Oh yeah, good point. The last thing we needed right now was a pumped-up Mike Manslaughter deciding to have us kicked out after all. I pulled my DJ Razz cap lower to hide my face.

As the band passed us a TV camera crew suddenly

appeared. They chased after Lethal Injection, filming the whole time.

"Hey," Deirdre said, dropping Frank's arm. "I should go wish Nick Needles good luck."

She raced after the TV crew. George rolled her eyes.

"Cameras are like a magnet to that girl," she muttered.

A moment later Lethal Injection, the TV cameras, and Deirdre had all disappeared from view. Nancy and I took the opportunity to fill in the others about our plan.

"I wish I could help out." Ned checked his watch. "But I'm already late getting back to work. I should be in the press tent right now, waiting my turn to interview the Royal We."

"Too bad, dude," I said. "See you."

I wasn't exactly heartbroken. Ned seemed like an okay guy, really. Maybe a little boring. I wondered how serious things were between him and Nancy. Maybe with Mr. Tall, Dark, and Studly out of the way for a while, I could find out.

Then again, maybe not. We might have our hands full trying to figure out the mystery mission.

"Okay," Frank said as soon as Ned was gone. "Joe and I will sneak backstage, and the rest of you can keep an eye on things out front."

Nancy frowned. "Nice try. The plan is to find the bad guys, not ditch the annoying girls."

Frank's cheeks went red. I hid a grin.

"How about this," I said. "Nancy and I will try to get backstage. The rest of you guys can blend in with the crowd."

I glanced at Frank. He didn't look happy, but he shrugged.

"Fine," he said. "Guess the three of us don't mind taking it easy and catching some tunes while you two take care of the hard stuff. Right, you guys?"

"Sure," Bess said.

George was staring after Lethal Injection. "Whatever," she said. "Let's hurry up, okay? I don't want to miss the band."

For a second, I was bummed. Why hadn't I thought of that? Now I was going to miss Lethal Injection.

Oh well. I would just have to deal. At least I would still be able to hear them.

We all headed back out front through the main gate. Luckily Tyreese was nowhere in sight. For some reason that guy really had it in for us.

We got out there just in time to see Lethal Injection's logo flash up on the big screens. The crowd let out a roar.

"Yeah!" I shouted, pumping my fist.

The air was electric. Everyone was surging forward,

trying to get as close as possible to the stage. The whole place felt alive, wired—and a little dangerous. In other words, it was awesome!

"Let's stick together until we find a good spot." Frank had to shout over the noise of the crowd. Up onstage the lights were going wild. Spotlights swooped around like drunken birds. The speakers emitted weird boops and whines and little bursts of minor chords.

It wasn't easy pushing our way through the crowd. Nobody wanted to give up their spot. We let Bess go first, which seemed to help. All the guys let us through, no problem, when they got a look at her.

Within minutes, we found ourselves in a decent spot off to the right, near the front. The lights were still swooping, the weird noises from the speakers were getting louder and weirder, and the crowd was working itself up into a frenzy. Beside me, George was jumping up and down for a better view.

"Yo, Mike Manslaughterrrrrr!" she screamed at the top of her lungs.

At that moment the stage suddenly went dark. The cheers increased.

Ka-pow!

Blinding white explosions burst up from the floor all across the front of the stage. A single guitar note screamed out of the speakers, so loud that I took a step back. Black smoke billowed out over the crowd.

Then came a familiar bass chord. Through the smoke, four figures could be seen leaping across the stage.

"Yeah!" I shouted. All around me other fans were screaming their lungs out. Even Frank let out a loud whistle.

The band immediately swung into one of their biggest hits, "Kill Me." It was loud and fast and a little loose, just like the best live music always is. I was totally loving it!

I jammed along with the song, for the moment not even caring that I was here on a mission. The music filled me up. I felt like a part of some huge organism, all of us focused on one thing.

Then the song ended. I raised both hands over my head and screamed for more along with everyone else.

Well, almost everyone. When I looked over at Frank, he was just standing there.

Did I mention my brother is a dweeb?

"Do you want to stay out here and watch?" he asked. He had to talk right into my ear so I could hear him. "I can go backstage with Nancy if you want."

"No way!" Just like that, the mission came back to me. "I'm on it."

"Good afternoon, Rockapazooma!" Mike Manslaughter screamed into the microphone. His crazy, raspy voice bounced out across the crowd, his yellow face filling the big screens over the stage and throughout the grounds. "Are you ready for a little death and destruction?"

Once again, the crowd went wild. "I hope they do 'Scream for Mercy' next!" George yelled in my ear.

But they didn't start another song. Instead Nick Needles swung down from behind his drums and stepped up to the microphone.

"What's going on?" I wondered.

"Hello, people." Nick's voice sounded a lot calmer than Mike's, just like it had back in the trailer. "Before we get back to the rock and roll, we want to take a minute to talk to you about the cause we're all supporting today."

"Oh, man," George muttered. "Like we could have missed it. They've only been showing that environmental stuff on the big screens all day."

"That's good," Nancy said. "This stuff is important. People need to hear it."

I shot her an appreciative glance. I like a girl with convictions.

"Come on," I told her. "Maybe we should get out of here while he's talking. Once the music starts, people will go nuts again."

"Good plan."

Frank stopped me with a hand on my arm. "Call me if you run into trouble."

I patted the cell phone in my pocket. "You know it, bro." I reached over and gave George a light punch on the arm. "Hey, enjoy the death scene," I said. "Even if you don't know what it's going to be."

George stuck out her tongue at me. I grinned and turned away.

Nancy and I started working our way around the stage. We were almost at the edge of the crowd when Nick Needles finished his speech and the band started their next song. George must have been thrilled—it was "Scream for Mercy."

"This way!" Nancy shouted at me over the music. She pointed off to the right. I could see why; there were a couple of green-shirted security guards just ahead.

We skirted them. The crowd was thinner out toward the edges of the stage. Soon only a few more guards stood between us and the speaker tower.

"Wow, there's a lot more security back here now," Nancy commented. "I wonder if that means something?"

"It means we'll have to work hard to get back there this time."

I wasn't kidding. There were at least a dozen guards spread out along the wings of the stage, and all of them looked like they meant business. How were we going to get past them?

Nancy must have been thinking the same thing.

"This doesn't look good," she shouted in my ear. "Maybe we need a plan B."

Now she was sounding like Frank, Mr. Backup Plan. Me, I don't believe in backup plans. We had to make this work somehow. . . .

"Dude!" A guy wandered up and poked me in the chest. "Hey, dude! Did you snag my cooler?"

"Huh?" I stared at him. He was chubby and kind of bloated-looking, like he'd had too much sun. And maybe too much beer, too. "What are you talking about?"

The guy scowled. "Don't lie to me, dude! I left it right there where you're standing. Blue cooler, white top."

Nancy stepped forward. "Sorry, you must be mistaken," she said. "We just got here."

"No, wait!" I said. I'd just had a brilliant idea. "Dude, I think I saw what happened. When we got here, this big guy wearing a hat was holding a blue cooler. He took off that way!" I pointed directly into the thickest part of the crowd.

"No way!" The guy looked outraged. "I'll teach him not to steal my stuff."

He raced off, swearing at the top of his lungs. Soon he'd disappeared into the crowd.

"What did you do that for?" Nancy frowned at me. "It wasn't very nice."

I grinned. "Just wait."

It didn't take long. Within a minute or two, there was a huge commotion from the direction the cooler guy had gone. The shouts and shrieks of outrage could be heard even over the music. All the security guards took off in that direction except for a couple. And they were so distracted by watching what was going on out there that they were barely paying attention.

I grabbed Nancy's arm. "Let's move!"

We took off toward the stage. Seconds later we were climbing across the lowest level of the speaker tower. The music was a little muffled back there, making it easier to hear.

"See? No Plan B required," I said.

"Hmm." Nancy didn't really answer that. I was pretty sure she was impressed, though, even if she wouldn't admit it. "So what now?"

I hadn't really thought that far ahead. But I wasn't about to say so.

I scooted forward a little, trying to get a view of the band. It was pretty cool seeing them from backstage. They'd just started another song, and Nick Needles was going crazy on the drums. I drummed along on my legs. My adrenaline was still pumping from sneaking in there, and there was no way I could sit still.

"Well?" Nancy sounded kind of impatient. "Should we try to get back to where the bands come through, or—"

"Let's climb up there." I pointed up the tower directly above us. "Try to get a good look around from up there."

"What? That makes no sense."

"Why not? We did it before."

"Yeah," Nancy said. "And you almost got caught. We won't be able to solve anything if we get kicked out of the show."

I rolled my eyes. Had she been taking buzz-kill lessons from Frank?

"We won't get caught," I told her. "Anyway, I don't hear you coming up with a better plan."

"Any plan is better than that," she countered. "What are we supposed to do if we spot the fake guards from up there? Fly down to chase them?"

It takes a lot to annoy me. But she was starting to get there.

"Look, all I'm saying is we climb up there and—"

I'd glanced up at the rigging above us while I was talking. As I did, I spotted movement up there. My mind flashed back to that guy who'd tried to kill us with the falling speaker earlier.

"Look out!" I shouted.

Pushing past Nancy, I jumped over a thick wad of wires and raced out onto the stage. I just hoped I wasn't too late. . . .

CHAPTER 14

NANCY

LESSON LEARNED

I spun around as Joe brushed past me. His eyes were practically popping out of his head. *"Look out!"* he yelled.

He ran out onto the stage, leaping over things in his way. Heading straight for the drum set at the back of the stage, he tackled Nick Needles, knocking him clear to the floor.

I gasped. What the . . . ?

A split second later, one of the enormous klieg lights that had been hanging overhead smashed down onto the drum set and exploded. The entire stage shuddered from the force of the crash, and the air popped and crackled with electricity. I ducked my head and covered my face with one arm as shattered glass sprayed everywhere.

Out front, as more sparks burst out from the wreckage, the crowd let out a "Wooooo!" It must have looked pretty spectacular from out there. From this close, though, it had been downright scary.

Sort of like an attempted murder.

I was thinking about all those discussions of Lethal Injection's murder/suicide gimmick. This had to be it, didn't it?

Joe was still rolling around on the stage with Nick Needles. Both of them appeared to be okay, although they were covered in slivers of glass from the gigantic lightbulb.

Wait a minute, I reminded myself, my mind clicking back into gear after the shock of what had just happened. *Joe claimed he and Frank were in on the big secret, so there are three possible explanations here. One, he was lying about that, and he just ruined the band's big death scene. Two, it was a terrible accident. Or three, this has something to do with that mission of theirs, or with the scar guys, or both.*

I carefully moved a little closer to the stage. My shoes crunched on broken glass, but I doubted anyone would hear. The speakers were emitting some kind of high-pitched feedback, and the crowd was screaming happily for more. Nobody out there seemed to suspect that a thing was wrong.

But I didn't share their viewpoint. All kinds of people were converging on Nick and Joe from different areas of the stage and the backstage area. And every one of them looked totally freaked out, including the other band members.

No. Definitely *not* planned, whatever the audience might think.

I glanced up, trying to see where the light had come from. As I did I caught a flash of neon green. Someone was clambering quickly along one of the catwalks at the top of the stage.

It had to be one of the fake guards. I raced past a bunch of speaker equipment toward the back corner of the stage, looking for a good spot to start climbing. But before I could, several security guards swarmed through the area. One of them, a bald guy with a pale, moon-shaped face, spotted me right away.

"You!" he barked out. "What are you doing back here?"

"Um . . . ," I began.

Just then I spotted a beautiful young woman rushing up behind him. She was petite and slender, with huge dark eyes and flawless brown skin. I gasped as I recognized her. It was Kijani!

"Come on!" she cried, sounding panicky as she pushed past the guard. Her soft, throaty, accented voice was almost lost in the commotion coming from the stage. "I must get to Nick!"

Okay, I thought, recalling the gossip Bess had mentioned the previous weekend. *I guess that tabloid was right. She and Nick Needles* are *dating.*

"Yes, miss," the guard said, but he grabbed my arm and dragged me along as he followed Kijani toward the stage. I had no choice but to go along—the guy was approximately the size of a Mack truck.

"Listen," I yelled to him. "There's a guy up there, in the rafters. I think he's an intruder. Maybe if someone can . . ."

My voice trailed off as I realized that the guard wasn't paying any attention to me at all. I might as well have been a piece of gum stuck to his shoe.

I looked up again. There was no longer any sign of Mr. Green Shirt.

By now we were out on the stage itself. It was hard to see what was going on through all the people. Glancing out at the audience, I saw that most people were still cheering, although a few near the front looked uncertain. When I checked one of the big screens along the side, I saw that it was showing more of the environmental interview videos, even though nobody was paying attention to them. At least *someone* in the control room seemed to have realized this wasn't part of the show.

I looked out toward the spot where Joe and I had

left the others. I couldn't see Bess and George at all, but I caught a glimpse of Frank pushing his way toward the stage.

"Nicky!" Kijani screamed.

Turning back to see what was going on, I saw the singer racing toward Nick. Several bodyguards leaped after her.

"Careful!" my guy shouted, dropping his hold on me. "Watch out for the glass!"

Free at last, I hurried closer to see if I could do anything to help. Now that I had a better view, I could see that Joe and Nick had been incredibly lucky. The huge metal casing of the light had landed directly on the drum set, smashing it to bits. Then it had bounced or rolled off to one side, coming to rest just three feet or so from where they'd ended up.

They were both sitting up by now, surrounded by people. Nick looked stunned; he was holding one hand to his forehead. His orange makeup was smeared, and his wig was lying on the stage beside him.

"Who's responsible for this?" Mike Manslaughter was screaming as I joined the circle of people around the pair. He was hopping up and down like an angry bantam rooster, shaking his fists at anyone and everyone. "I demand an answer! Nicky could've been killed!"

Joe looked up and spotted me. His face was pale and serious. There was a smudge of orange makeup on his chin. I wanted to go over to him, but one of the green-shirted security guards was holding people back.

"Give them some space," he said. "Let the doctor check them over."

A woman carrying a first-aid kit had just appeared in the circle. She crouched down beside Nick, talking quietly to him.

I glanced around, wondering if I could get a little closer to that fallen light. At least a dozen guards were all around me, most of them huddling around the two guys and the doctor, or standing in a line behind all of us to block the audience's view of the stage. I also saw that I was standing right next to the other two members of Lethal Injection. I didn't know their names, but one was wearing purple stage makeup while the other was all in electric blue.

"'Ow'd somethin' like this 'appen, then?" Purple asked Blue in a strong Cockney accent.

"Dunno." Blue shook his head. "But Mikey's gonna have someone's head over it, just watch. Never seen him so upset."

I ducked behind them, moving closer to the smashed light fixture. This could be my only chance to check it out for anything suspicious. As soon as the guards noticed I didn't belong, I'd be out of there.

When I reached the light casing, I was even more amazed that Joe and Nick Needles had escaped serious injury or worse. The thing was enormous. The bulb was totally gone, smashed into smithereens from the impact. Even the metal part was twisted, and there were several gouges in the wooden stage floor.

I stepped around it, trying to get a look at the cable that had connected it to the rigging. Before I got back there, I spotted something small and white flapping from one of the thin metal frame pieces.

Leaning closer, I saw that it was a slip of paper that had been attached to the frame with wire. It had writing on it—a note?

I didn't want to touch anything before the police got there, so I just leaned as close as I could to try to read it. But there was a breeze blowing across the open air stage, and the thing kept waving around. I managed to make out a snippet in the middle—"teach you a lesson about interfering with the sovereign rights of"—before something else caught my eye: a flash of neon green from behind a speaker nearby!

I spun around for a better look. Sure enough, a figure was back there. Unlike the guards onstage, who were bustling around out in the open, this one was lurking just out of sight. I couldn't see his face from where I was standing, but I was sure it had to be one of the scar twins.

"Hey!" I yelled. "Look back there! Somebody grab that guy, quick!"

In the chaos still going on around me, I only managed to catch the attention of one guard. Unfortunately it was the guy who'd grabbed me backstage.

"You still here?" he growled, lurching toward me. "Time to show me your credentials, or you're out of here."

"No, wait!" I said, struggling as he dragged me off toward the side of the stage. "Listen to me for a second. You have to catch that guy. I think he's the one who did this!"

I turned to point out the bad guy. But there was no sign of him.

"Nice try," the real guard said.

"Hold on! I'll go, but please, just make sure someone takes a look at that note, okay? It's tied to the light that fell."

"Note?" Sounding interested in what I was saying for the first time, the guard stopped and looked back. "What note?"

"It's right there on the side of the light," I said. "You can't miss it."

He dragged me back a few steps. He was still holding me by the upper arm, so I couldn't turn around to point out the note myself. Instead I watched his face, which I could see by twisting my neck around.

I saw him frown. "Okay, you almost got me that time, missy," he snapped. "I don't know what you're trying to pull, but you're not getting any closer to the band."

"No, I swear! I just saw it!" I wriggled hard enough to break loose for a second. Spinning around, I stared at the light fixture.

But the note was gone.

CHAPTER 15

FRANK

SLIPPING AWAY

"Nice meeting spot you picked here, Frank," Joe said. "Very fragrant."

I was glad to see his recent brush with death hadn't affected his sense of humor. It was as lame as ever.

All five of us—Joe, Nancy, Bess, George, and me—were standing behind a long row of Porta-Johns near the food area. Joe had called on his cell as soon as the people up onstage had released him. I'd gone back and grabbed Bess and George and headed for the closest quiet spot I could find.

Yeah, that would be Toilet Row. So sue me.

Once we were there, I called Joe back and told him where to meet us. I guess he picked up Nancy somewhere along the way—George tried to call her, but it turned out Nancy wasn't even carrying a phone.

By the time we were all together again nearly half an hour had passed. Needless to say, Lethal Injection hadn't finished their set. But the video guys had worked fast, putting up some interviews and stuff on the big screens to entertain people while the cleanup crew did their thing.

Soon the broken glass and stuff had been swept off most of the stage, and there were a bunch of screens up to block everyone's view of the fallen light and smashed drum set. Then Mack-Daddy had come onstage to assure everyone the light thing had been an accident, and another artist, Cherry Pye, had taken the stage.

"So did you get to meet all the Lethal Injection guys?" George asked Joe and Nancy.

"Not exactly," Nancy replied. "We were kind of busy."

"Yeah, busy trying not to die," Joe said. He was bopping and tapping his foot to Cherry Pye's song, a dance hit from about six months ago. "Did you guys see the size of that light? One more second, and Nick Needles would've been toast."

Nancy took a step toward him, peering at his head. "Hold still," she ordered. "You still have glass in your hair."

Joe stopped dancing and ducked his head down. Nancy reached up and brushed her hand through his bangs.

"Thanks," Joe said, shooting her a look.

Uh-oh. I recognized that look. It meant trouble.

Trouble with a capital G-I-R-L.

This mission was rapidly spinning out of control. Okay, so we started out not knowing what we were doing there. Fine. I could handle that. It only made our task more challenging, and there's nothing I like more than a challenge.

Then we accidentally gave away our identity to a random bunch of girls.

Wait. Scratch that. *Joe* gave away our identity to a random bunch of girls.

And as if that's not bad enough, one of those girls happened to be an amateur detective. One who'd actually heard of ATAC.

We just couldn't get a break.

Now this light thing had happened. Suddenly this mission was starting to look serious. Deadly serious. And I was getting really worried about letting these amateurs play in the big leagues with us.

The others were still chattering about the incident. "So what do you think happened?" Bess was asking Nancy and Joe. "Could it have been an accident?"

"No way," Joe said. "I saw a guy up there right before that light fell. He was wearing one of those bright green shirts like the guards have. And when he leaned over the front of the light, I saw that big scar Nancy was talking about. When I saw the light start to sway, I figured out what he was up to. I mean, Frank and I saw the rehearsal for the death scene, so I knew it didn't have anything to do with stuff falling from up there."

I nodded. That guy Nick Needles was lucky Joe was there and paying attention. Otherwise the whole concert would have ended in tragedy.

"I'm pretty sure I saw the guy too," Nancy said. "At least twice. Or maybe it was the other scar guy, I don't know. He was lurking around up in the speaker tower right after the light fell. Then later I saw him hiding at the back of the stage. He must have jumped out and grabbed that note I saw while I was arguing with the real security guard."

"Note? What note?" I asked.

"Try to keep up, bro." Joe shot me a strange look. "She just went through all that, like, two minutes ago."

I vaguely remembered Nancy saying something about a clue. But I hadn't been paying much attention. That was about the time I was realizing that Joe and I could easily get these girls killed if we let them keep tagging along with us. They were just too distracting.

"I spotted a note on the light fixture," Nancy told me. "It sounded like a warning, at least from the little I saw. Something about teaching someone a lesson about interfering in something."

Joe rubbed one hand through his hair, probably still checking for glass. "All along I figured this mission would turn out to be about bootleg concert tapes or whatever. But that doesn't seem big enough to explain all the secrecy."

Nancy looked thoughtful. "Is it possible Lethal Injection sued someone for bootlegging one of their shows? Maybe aggravated the wrong person?"

"Nice theory, but nope." George shook her head. "In fact, they totally encourage their fans to download their bootlegs from the Internet." She grinned. "It really gets the record companies mad."

"So maybe that's the answer," Bess suggested. "Maybe the record companies have had enough of the band's attitude and want to teach them a lesson."

"What kind of record company handles problems with its artists by dropping huge lights on them?" Nancy shook her head. "No, I think it's time to start thinking outside the box."

I definitely agreed with her on that. Enough was enough. And it was time to cut the girls loose so Joe and I could get on with the mission.

"Excuse me," I said. "I'll be right back. Nature calls."

I hooked a thumb at the Porta-Johns. The others barely glanced at me.

"We'll be right here," Joe said. Then he returned his attention to the girls. "What about drugs?" he said. "I wonder if . . ."

I didn't stick around to hear any more. I walked to the

toilets, but I didn't stop there. I headed toward the back of the stage. It was still pretty busy back there. Roadies and other official-looking people were rushing around, and a pair of uniformed police officers were talking to several security guards near the backstage passageway.

I headed the opposite way. There was a tall stack of those metal crowd barricades nearby. Ducking behind it, I pulled out my phone and hit speed dial #1.

"Yo," Joe's voice answered. "Frank, is that you? You need me to bring you some TP or what?"

"It's me." I ignored the TP comment. "Listen, you need to sneak away from those girls."

"What? Why?"

"Don't be an idiot. Things are getting dangerous—we can't risk their lives."

"Oh." There was a long pause. I could hear one of the girls saying something in the background, although I couldn't make it out. Then Joe's voice came again, a little distant this time. "Oh, that's just Frank," he said. "He's a little claustrophobic. He tends to panic when he's locked inside a Porta Potti."

I rolled my eyes. Thanks, bro.

Then he came back on the line. "Fine," he said. "Talk to me."

"I'm behind the stage." I quickly gave him a more detailed description of my location. "So just make an excuse and get here. Hurry."

"Got it."

The line went dead. I closed the phone and stuck it back in my pocket. Then I checked my watch. The concert was a little behind schedule now. Even so, it would be over in a little more than two hours. We were going to have to step it up if we wanted to get anywhere on this mission.

I was pacing back and forth in front of the barricades when Joe came jogging up fifteen minutes later. "About time," I greeted him.

"Hey, cut me a break," he said breathlessly. "Nancy and her friends aren't easy to lose. I had to tell them I was getting dehydrated from the heat so I could pretend to go off and buy a drink. George is probably still waiting for that root beer I promised to pick up for her." He frowned at me. "I don't see why we had to ditch them. In case you hadn't noticed, they were actually trying to help us figure this thing out."

It was obvious he wasn't happy about being dragged away from his new friends. But I didn't have much sympathy.

"Look, we need to find that guy with the scar," I said.

"Guys," Joe corrected. "There are two of them, remember?"

"Whatever." I still wasn't convinced of that. It seemed a lot more likely that Nancy was mistaken about the different scars than that there were twin thugs running around. "Him, them—either way it's our only real lead so far."

Joe nodded. "So far we've always spotted them near the stage. We might as well start looking here."

"Fine." I hated not having a better plan than that. But there didn't seem to be much choice.

The cops had disappeared, so we wandered along behind the stage. I kept a sharp eye out for anyone or anything out of the ordinary. Joe was eyeing the speaker towers again.

"Hey," he said. "Maybe we should climb up there and see if we can—"

"No," I interrupted. "We don't need a better look at the grounds. What we need is to stay focused and find that guy. Guys," I added quickly before he could correct me.

"Whatever."

I veered over toward the chain-link fence separating where we were from the trailer and bus area beyond. That way, I figured, we could watch both places at once.

We were getting closer to our secret sneak-through in the fence. I wondered if we should go back there again. If the bad guy had a security T-shirt, it seemed likely he could gain access to anywhere on the concert grounds. What if he sneaked back into the trailers and tried to hurt the Lethal Injection guys again, or maybe one of the other artists?

Suddenly Joe's eyes widened. He pointed off toward a cluster of Dumpsters along the fence just ahead.

"There he is!" he shouted.

I spun around just in time to see a flash of neon green disappearing behind the Dumpsters. Joe was already sprinting that way.

"Joe, wait!" I cried. Rushing around like idiots hadn't worked very well so far. Maybe if we stopped for half a second to come up with a plan . . .

But he didn't stop. Grumbling under my breath, I took off after him.

I caught up just as he rounded the corner of the first Dumpster. A burly, green-shirted man was back there. He was bending down to pick up something from the ground, so I couldn't see his face. But the bulging muscles and dark skin of his arms matched Nancy's description.

"Hey!" Joe shouted. As he leaped forward, I saw that he had his mini-cattle-prod in one hand.

I reached in and pulled out mine, too, my heart thumping. Maybe this wasn't the way I would've done it. But we had him! With the help of our devices, there was no way the mystery guard was getting away from us this time!

ZZZZZZAP!

The electric sizzle of Joe's device echoed off the metal sides of the Dumpster. Mr. Green Shirt yelped in surprise and pain and went down hard.

He rolled over on his back, clutching his shoulder where Joe had zinged him. I jumped forward, ready to apply a second dose if he needed it.

Then I stopped short. "Um, Joe . . ." I began with a gulp.

The guy writhing in pain didn't have a scar on his head. But he did have a familiar face. Way too familiar.

"Dude," Joe whispered, sounding horrified. "It's Tyreese!"

I froze, not knowing what to do. The big guard already had it in for us. If he snapped out of it in time to spot us now . . .

As if on cue, Tyreese opened his eyes. It took him a second to focus, but when he frowned, I knew he'd recognized us.

"You two!" he cried in a strangled voice. He rolled over and shoved himself to his feet.

"Run!" Joe shouted.

But it was too late. Tyreese lurched forward and grabbed us both.

"Hand them over, boys." His voice was already returning to its normal threatening rumble. I guess those prod thingies aren't meant to tackle a dude that big.

We handed over our mini-cattle-prods. What choice did we have? Did I mention the guy was huge?

Tyreese stuck the gadgets in his pocket. "All right, boys," he said grimly. "Let's go."

NANCY

CHAPTER 16

DISAPPEARANCES

"I still can't believe they ditched us," I grumbled.

"Believe it," George advised. "I could tell those two were shady right from the start."

Bess laughed. "No, you couldn't," she said. "They aren't shady at all. I'm sure they think they're just keeping us safe by running off like that."

She was probably right. The Hardys did seem like nice guys. Sure, Frank was a little uptight, and Joe a bit spazzy. But both of them were smart and obviously dedicated to their work with ATAC. I could even understand why they'd given us the slip.

That didn't mean I was going to let them get away with it.

"They're obviously not here in the food stands. Let's

check over near the stage," I said. We'd been searching for any sign of the Hardys ever since it had become clear that the guys weren't coming back.

"We can try." George glanced that way, looking dubious. "If we can get near it."

She had a point. A singer named Cherry Pye had just finished her set, and the popular alt-rock/hip-hop fusion band the Angst Gangstas was up next. Even as Mack-Daddy began his introduction, just about everyone in the audience under the age of twenty-five was crushing closer to the stage.

"Okay, maybe we should look *behind* the stage," I said. "It might be a little easier to get around back there."

George shot a wistful look at the stage as Mack-Daddy explained that the Angst Gangstas would be out in just a few minutes. "Man, it would be nice to actually *see* some of this concert before it's over," she said. "Not to mention, I never did get my root beer."

"Come on," Bess told her. "You know Nancy's not going to give up when there's any kind of mystery happening. And we certainly can't let her run off by herself."

"We can't?" George retorted. But she trailed along as Bess and I pushed our way through a throng of excited younger teens toward the corner of the stage.

I glanced up at the speaker tower as we reached it. It

seemed like it had been ages since I'd climbed up there to chase the fake guard. It *had* been ages. The concert only had a few more acts to go. After the big finale by the Royal We, it would be over. We didn't have much time to find the Hardys and get the mystery sorted out.

"Wait," George said from behind me. "Isn't that Deirdre on the big screen?"

Bess and I stopped and turned. George was right. Deirdre's familiar smug smile was plastered across all the video screens within view. A second later, Annie Wu flashed up in her place.

"Here I am with a big fan of the environment," the VJ said. "Which act are you most psyched to see today?"

Deirdre flashed back up on the video screen. "Definitely the Royal We. See, I know Kijani really well, and she's an awesome person," screen-Deirdre said. "She's totally all about the environment."

The shot jumped to a pimply-faced boy in a black T-shirt. "I was totally geeked to see LI," he exclaimed. "I never thought much about the environment until I heard Mike Manslaughter do an interview about the rain forest. . . ."

"That must have been Deirdre's big interview with Annie Wu," Bess said. "Remember? She pushed her way in front of us right after we rescued her from that guy."

"Oh, I remember it, all right." George grinned. "Bet she's not happy that they cut her off after one second. Knowing Deirdre, she probably thought they'd turn her interview into a miniseries or something."

"At least she got in the part about being best pals with Kijani." Bess giggled. "That's obviously the main thing she wants everybody in the world to know."

After flashing to two or three more interview snippets, the screen suddenly went blank. Then the Angst Gangstas' latest album cover flashed up there. The crowd let out a collective shriek.

"Come on, let's keep moving," I said. The ADHD-style editing on the video feed was giving me a headache. Besides, we were still no closer to finding the Hardys, let alone the scar brothers. And time was running out.

Out of the corner of my eye, I saw Mack-Daddy step toward the microphone again. "And now, without further ado," he began. He waved an arm and the Angst Gangstas capered out of the wings.

The crowd went crazy. But we didn't stick around to watch. By the time the band was halfway through their first number, we were halfway across the open area behind the stage.

"Here we are, back where we started," George said, tapping her thigh with one hand along with the pulsing beat from out front. She nodded toward the gate leading back to the trailer and press area.

I remembered the Hardys' secret entrance back there and looked for it. There it was—and at the moment there were no guards in sight.

"Come on," I said, hurrying that way. "Let's go find Ned. Maybe he's seen the Hardys."

Once we were in, we headed straight over toward the press tent. We got there just in time to see Ned burst out of it, trailed by none other than Deirdre Shannon.

"Can you believe how they butchered my interview?" she was complaining at the top of her lungs. "I mean, Ned, you're a professional journalist, right? Just tell me that wasn't the most pathetic thing you ever saw!"

"I already told you I didn't see it, Deirdre."

To anyone else Ned probably sounded as patient as ever. But I knew him well enough to tell that he was at the end of his rope. And no wonder, if Deirdre had been following him around. She could try the patience of a robot.

"Well, you're lucky you missed it." Deirdre shook her head and stuck her lower lip out in a pout. "It was horrible. They barely let me get two words out before they cut away!"

"That's too bad." Ned glanced at his watch. "Now if you'll excuse me . . . Nancy!" His face lit up as he spotted me walking toward him.

That's the kind of thing that always makes a girl feel good. "Hi there," I greeted him, hurrying forward with Bess and George at my heels. "How's everything going back here?"

"Not so great, actually," Ned said. "I was supposed to interview Kijani, like, half an hour ago, and she's a no-show. If she doesn't get here soon, we may have to—"

"I'm sure Kijani is busy," Deirdre broke in. "Her boyfriend just practically got killed, remember? I'm sure she forgot all about your little interview." She glanced around at us. "Hey, what happened to your cute friends? Especially that guy Frank? I thought he seemed too cool to be hanging around with you guys."

"Funny you should ask," George retorted. "He saw you coming and decided to go kill him—"

Deirdre didn't let her finish. "Hey, there's one of Annie Wu's camera guys!" she exclaimed. "Maybe he can tell me if they're planning on actually showing the rest of my interview."

She raced off without a backward glance. George rolled her eyes. "Well, now we know the Hardys can't be anywhere within a fifty-foot radius," she said. "Otherwise, DeeDee's boy-spotting radar would've picked up the signal in seconds."

"Hey," Ned said. "What *did* happen to those guys?"

"Good question." I was about to explain, but just

then a woman in a business suit hurried out of the press tent calling Ned's name.

"Kijani's on her way," the woman said breathlessly, jabbing one manicured finger at the little stage set-up nearby. "You're up first. Be ready."

"I'm on it." Ned shot me an apologetic glance. "Gotta go."

My friends and I backed up out of the way as Ned stepped over to the interview area. A moment later, Kijani arrived with a sizable entourage. In addition to half a dozen imposing-looking security guards, she was accompanied by several people in suits and a young woman who was working away busily on Kijani's black curls as they walked.

"So sorry I am late!" Kijani called to Ned. Even out of breath, her voice sounded husky and musical, her exotic accent only adding to its charm. She stepped out of reach of her hairdresser and stuck out her hand toward Ned. "I am sure you heard about what happened during Lethal Injection's set. I'm afraid I was so worried over poor Nick that I lost track of the time. My deepest apologies to you, Mr. Nickerson."

"That's exactly what I was trying to tell him, Kijani!" a voice called out.

I turned to see that Deirdre had reappeared. She was trying to push her way through Kijani's people, craning her neck to see past one of the bodyguards.

"She's ba-a-ack," George said softly in a singsong voice.

Kijani shot Deirdre a slightly confused-looking smile. Then she turned back to Ned.

"Now, shall we have our interview?" she asked Ned with a charming tilt of her head.

"Of course. Thanks for your time, Kijani," Ned said. The two of them stepped into the cordoned-off interview area a few feet away. "You don't mind if I call you Kijani, do you?"

"Of course not!" The singer chuckled. "That is, after all, my name."

Deirdre let out a shriek of laughter. "Good one, Kijani!" she yelled.

I glanced at her again. By now she'd been shuffled back by the crowd and was pressed up against the corner of a large beige trailer.

George was looking too. "Check her out," she hissed at Bess and me, sounding amused. "You can tell Kijani has no clue who she is. So much for being best friends!"

I chuckled, but I wasn't that interested in Deirdre's delusions of secondhand celebrity. Seeing her had only reminded me how important it was to find the Hardy brothers and continue our investigation. Otherwise, we might never know who had grabbed Deirdre and dropped that light on Lethal Injection, let alone why they'd done it.

". . . and so I do try to tell people the truth about what has happened in my country," Kijani was telling Ned, a somber expression on her lovely face. The watching crowd was silent as everyone listened to her, making it easy to hear from where we were standing. "It was a terrible, terrible thing. I am not ashamed to name the bad men who have caused it, to denounce them to the world. But as terrible as it was, it is only one tiny country in Africa that has been affected by the coup. The destruction of our environment, however, is something that affects everyone, in every land. That is why I speak out so much more about . . ."

I leaned closer to Bess. "Maybe we should head out," I whispered. "Go scout around back in the trailer rows, or—"

"Hey!" George cried, interrupting. She clutched at my arm and gave it a yank. "Someone just grabbed Deirdre!"

One look at her face made me realize she wasn't kidding around. "What happened?"

"She was standing there, laughing like a loon at whatever Kijani just said," George said. "Then this guy popped out from behind that trailer, put a hand over her mouth, and pulled her back there with him."

"Come on!" I led the way in the direction of the last spot I'd seen Deirdre. It took a few moments to get there through the audience that had gathered to watch Kijani's interview, but finally we broke free of the crowd and rushed around the corner of the beige trailer.

There was no sign of life back there. When I glanced at the dirt, though, I saw the imprints of several heavy footsteps, along with the several gouges that looked like they could have been caused by a scuffle.

Bess stared down at the marks. "Maybe a real security guard got tired of Deirdre causing a ruckus backstage and kicked her out," she suggested uncertainly.

"What kind of real guard would cover her mouth and drag her behind a trailer?" My heart sank as I realized what this meant. "No way. I think this time, Deirdre really has been kidnapped!"

CHAPTER 17

JOE

AN UNPLEASANT SURPRISE

Frank was waiting for me near the backstage fence. He did *not* look happy.

"Nice work, brother," he said with a frown. "Way to keep a low profile."

I grinned, glancing up at the nearest video screen. My own face grinned back at me, frozen up there like a giant color poster of me. A second later it faded out, replaced by the gorgeous face of Annie Wu.

"Hey, what can I say?" I told Frank. "When someone like Annie asks me to say a few words, I can't say no."

"Yeah," Frank muttered. "I've noticed." He sighed loudly and shook his head. "In case you've forgotten, we're here to do a job. We're not here to try to get on TV.

What if the bad guys spotted you and figured out who you were?"

"Lighten up, man," I said. "It's not like we're accomplishing much on the mission so far, anyway. We've just been wandering around in circles for the past hour since we got away from our buddy Ty."

Oh, right. You're probably wondering how we escaped being kicked out of the show by Tyreese, right? Well, just about the time he was dragging us toward the exit, we passed those cops who'd come to investigate the LI incident. That's when I remembered that, for once, we weren't sworn to absolute secrecy about being there with ATAC. We got one of the cops to call in to HQ and confirm that we needed to be there.

Tyreese wasn't happy about letting us go. And Frank wasn't happy about blowing our cover, even though the mission CD said it was okay to go to the cops for help if necessary. But there we were—no real harm done.

Not that Frank agreed with me.

"Maybe all *you've* been doing is wandering around. *I've* been searching for those scar guys," he said.

I tapped my foot along with the band now playing onstage, a bunch of classic-rock type dudes who had to be at least fifty. My interview had aired during a break between their songs. I guess they were old enough to need the rest.

"Okay, whatever," I told Frank. "But chill, okay? It's

not like anyone who saw that interview knows I'm an ATAC agent."

"Nobody?" Frank said, his face grim. "What about—"

"Frank! Joe! There you are!"

I spun around. Nancy was rushing toward us, with her two friends right behind her. They skidded to a stop in front of us.

"Um, hi," I said, forcing a weak smile. "There you guys are. We've been looking everywhere."

"Very funny." Nancy crossed her arms and glared. "Care to explain why you decided to ditch us?"

For a second, my only rational thought was that she looked even cuter when she was angry. The flushed face, the annoyed expression, the slightly messy hair—it all added up to a serious ten-plus for me. Did that make me a freak?

"Look, it was for your own good," Frank said. "We didn't want to put you guys in any more danger, so we decided it was best just to slip away."

Just then the classic rock guys onstage finished their song. We couldn't see the stage from where we were, but there were video screens all over the place. A second later Mack-Daddy appeared on them.

"Bear with us, folks," he cried. "Our terrific crew just needs a few minutes for a set change. And then we'll all get to enjoy today's headliners—the fabulous and talented Royal We!"

Out in front of the stage, the crowd cheered wildly. We pretty much ignored it, though. We were all still staring one another down like two sets of cowboys in an old Western.

George smirked at Frank. "If you wanted to keep a low profile, it was really brilliant of you to do a live interview up on the big screen," she said. "Good thing Bess happened to look up at the right moment, or we might have missed it."

"Yeah." Nancy let out a short, angry-sounding laugh. "And it was especially helpful that you were standing right in front of that weird spot in the fence. That way we knew exactly where to look for you."

"Nice work, detective," I joked.

Talk about major bad luck. They must have been close by when they spotted me up on the screen and recognized that spot in the fence. Otherwise it would have taken them ages rather than minutes to get to us through the crowd.

Still, if fate was determined to throw us back together, I, for one, was ready to live with it. Frank didn't look quite so ready, though.

"In case you didn't notice, *I* wasn't up on that screen," he began, glancing up at the closest video screen. It was showing more of Annie Wu's audience interviews. "That was my brilliant brother, all on his own."

Nancy shushed him with a wave of her hand. "Whatever; it doesn't matter. Something big just happened," she said. "It's Deirdre—I think they got her this time."

"What?" I said.

"Tell us," Frank ordered.

"We were back there." Nancy waved a hand toward the trailer area. "Deirdre was nearby. Then George saw somebody grab her."

George nodded. "It was a big guy in a brown jacket."

"One of those scar guys?" I asked.

She shrugged. "Couldn't tell," she said. "He had a hat pulled down over his face. Plus I only saw him for, like, a tenth of a second."

"We ran over there, but we couldn't see anyone," Nancy added.

Bess looked worried. "We have to find her!"

"We're on it." Frank was all business now—no more whining about splitting up. "Take us to where you saw her last."

That turned out to be easier said than done. There were two security guards at that hole in the fence.

For once I would have been glad to see Tyreese. At least now he knew better than to get in our way, even if he still didn't know exactly why. But these dudes were strangers. And they didn't look friendly.

"Never mind," Nancy said as we turned away. "I

already took a look at the crime scene. The only clue was a couple of footprints."

"We need to figure out where he took her," Frank said.

"How can we know that if we don't even know *why* he took her?" George asked.

She had a point. We still had no idea what those goons wanted with some small-town rich girl.

"He's probably holed up on the grounds somewhere," I guessed.

Frank looked thoughtful. "But if he's not . . ."

"We should split up and check the exits," Nancy said. She pointed to me. "Joe and I can run over to the main gate. The rest of you, check out the back entrance, okay?"

"Good plan." This time Frank didn't bother to argue about who got to do what. "Come on, guys, let's go."

Soon I was jogging across the grounds beside Nancy. I was psyched that she'd decided to pick me to be on her team again.

Guess she can't resist the ol' Joe charm, I thought. *And no wonder. She'd have to be impressed, seeing me jump out and save Nick Needles like that, with no thought for my own—*

"I hope Deirdre's okay," Nancy said, interrupting my thoughts. "She's got to be terrified."

"So tell me more about this Deirdre chick," I said as we ran. "Why would someone want to kidnap her?"

"I've been asking myself the same question all day." Nancy dodged a food stand in our path. "I mean, her family's pretty well-to-do. But they're not Rockefeller rich or anything. Besides, how often do people actually get kidnapped for ransom these days?"

"No clue. But what other motive could there be? If these dudes just wanted to snag themselves a cute girl, there are plenty to choose from around here. They obviously wanted *her*. But why?"

She looked troubled. "Her dad's law firm represents a lot of multinational companies and stuff. I wonder if this could have something to do with one of his international cases?"

"Huh?" The lawyer-dad thing made sense, but for a second I wasn't sure where she was getting the international part. Then I remembered: the accent. "Wait, what kind of accent do those scar guys have, anyway?"

"Oh, man," Nancy murmured, slowing almost to a stop. "I just realized . . . Joe, we have to go see if we can talk to Kijani!"

I slowed down too. We were almost at the main entrance gate by now.

"What are you talking about?" I asked.

Before she could answer, the sound system suddenly cut out in the middle of one of those audience interviews. The sudden silence was kind of freaky. A murmur went up from the crowd.

Nancy stopped and glanced back toward the stage. "What happened?"

I shrugged. The video screens had gone dark too. "Technical difficulties?" I guessed.

Any reply she might have made was drowned out by a sudden, eardrum-shattering scream of feedback. Whoever was working the sound system must have turned it up to eleven.

My head was still ringing when the screens burst back to life. A close-up of a pretty girl's face filled them.

"Hey," I said. "Isn't that—"

"Deirdre!" Nancy cried.

She barely looked like the same girl. Deirdre's face was streaked with tears, and her lipstick was smudged. She looked totally freaked out.

"Help me!" she sobbed, her voice ringing out at top volume over the concert grounds. "Please!"

"What the . . . ?" I murmured.

Onscreen, Deirdre was still speaking. "Someone, please tell Kijani she has to come to the stage right now," she wailed. "Otherwise they're going to kill me!"

CHAPTER 18

NANCY

STAGE FRIGHT

The whole place went crazy. People started screaming and running around. Others were laughing and cheering, clearly assuming this was some kind of prank.

But Joe and I knew it was deadly serious. "If they want Kijani up on the stage, they may be holding Deirdre there too," he said. "We've got to get back there and see what's going on."

I didn't have time to react to that before Joe's cell phone rang. He whipped it out.

"Frank? Did you guys see that?" Joe paused and listened for a moment, nodding several times. "Okay, we're on it," he said at last.

He hung up. "They're going to try to get onstage,"

he said. "We're supposed to find Kijani and try to figure out what's up from that angle."

"Exactly what I was thinking."

The two of us raced back the way we'd just come. We reached the backstage passage behind the stage just in time to see Kijani running toward it from the other side. Her face was twisted in an anguished expression. Several of her bodyguards were running after her, calling frantically for her to stop.

"I have to go out there!" she cried back to them without slowing her pace. "That girl, she is innocent. She is in danger because of me!"

Now that she was upset, her accent was stronger than usual. I could have kicked myself when I heard it again. Why hadn't I made the connection sooner?

"Let me through, please!" Kijani cried as she reached the gate.

Most of the people standing around obeyed, but I jumped forward, grabbed the singer's arm, and spun her to face me. I figured one of the bodyguards would rush over and knock me senseless pretty soon, so I talked fast.

"Listen to me," I told her. "We know that girl on the video. If you tell us what's going on, maybe we can help."

Kijani tugged against my grip, seeming distracted. "I can't let this happen," she exclaimed. "Please, let me go! I cannot let an innocent stranger suffer for my problems."

The bodyguards moved toward me. One grabbed me by the arm. "Come with us, miss," he rumbled in a deep voice.

"But you can't just run out there," I told Kijani, struggling against the guard. "These people are obviously crazy. What do they want with you, anyway? Are they from your home country?"

Beside me, Joe let out a low whistle. "Dude!" he murmured. "The accent!"

I ignored him. I was still staring into Kijani's face. "Please," I said urgently. "There's no time to explain, but we want to help."

Something about my plea must have convinced her. She waved the guards back, and they dropped their grip on me. "It is the Death Brothers," she said softly. "I should have known they would find a way to get to me."

"The who?" Joe stepped forward. "Who are the Death Brothers?"

"They are very bad men." Kijani shook her head sadly. "They are thugs and killers. They work for Abrafo, the man who took over my country. At least they *did*."

"What do you mean?" I asked.

"When Abrafo and his gang of thugs reached the capital, he intended to kill my parents," Kijani said. "He sent his favorite assassins to find them and bring them to him to be executed."

"The Death Brothers?" Joe guessed.

"Exactly. They have caused much grief and suffering all over Africa." Kijani closed her eyes briefly, her expression haunted. "But this time they failed. My parents and I were able to escape. And the brothers were lucky to escape too, with only those scars as their punishment."

I shuddered. I didn't want to imagine the kind of "punishment" that would cause those scars.

Kijani sighed. "As long as my parents live, the world is reminded that Abrafo is nothing but a thug himself, an illegitimate dictator with no rights to rule Urdzania. That is why he still wants them dead. But they have good friends who protect them in their new home in Europe." She glanced over at her watchful bodyguards. "As you can see, I have protection too."

"Okay, but I thought the Death Brothers were on the outs with this dictator," Joe said. "Why are they still after you?"

"They hope Abrafo will welcome them back if they bring me to him," Kijani replied. "With me as his prisoner, he knows my parents will do whatever he demands. This is not the first time they have tried to reach me throughout the past two years, but as I said, I am very well protected. I suppose they have finally figured out that my fans may be easier targets." She glanced down at her hands, which were twisted in front of her. "We knew that the Death Brothers would never give up. But I never guessed it would happen like this." Her dark eyes filled with tears, but she blinked them back. "Please," she said. "I must go now. That girl does not deserve to be a pawn in this terrible game. No innocent person does."

"Okay, but wait," Joe said. "I get that these assassin dudes can't get to you directly, so they're trying to make you turn yourself over to them in exchange for their innocent prisoner. But why this Deirdre girl in particular? They've been after her all day."

I'd just figured out the answer to that. It was all starting to make sense now. The Death Brothers were trying to scare Kijani by terrorizing everyone close to her—they would do anything, from trying to kill her boyfriend in front of a live audience to kidnapping someone they *believed* was her friend. "Because they thought she was Kijani's best friend," I said. "Deirdre's been telling everyone who will listen how close the two of them are."

Now it was Kijani's turn to look confused. "I am sorry?" she said. "I do not understand. The girl on the screens—I do not know her."

That figured. Deirdre wasn't the type to out-and-out lie, but she *was* willing to stretch the truth to the breaking point at times. She'd probably run into Kijani somewhere or other and begged her for her autograph, and turned that brief meeting into her stories of close friendship.

But there was no time to ponder the possibilities further. Kijani was already pulling away from me. "I must go," she said, her voice cracking with emotion. "I will do what must be done."

"No, wait," I said. I was horrified that the singer was actually thinking of giving in to the bad guys' demands. "Please, give us a chance to fix this first."

"You do not understand," Kijani said. "These men, they will kill you as easily as they swat a fly."

"Trust me, I understand." Joe glanced at me. "We're not ordinary teenagers. We—we're sort of trained for this stuff."

She still didn't seem convinced, and neither did her bodyguards. But just then a green-shirted security guard stepped toward us. He looked sort of familiar.

His name tag read TYREESE. That jogged my memory. It was the guy who'd barred Deirdre from backstage. And also the one who'd mistaken Bess for Toni Lovely.

"Excuse me," he rumbled in a deep voice. "I couldn't help overhearing what you all were talking about. Ms. Kijani, these kids aren't what you think they are." He shot Joe a slightly disgruntled glance. "I'm not sure *what* they are, but I think they might be able to help."

"Ty! Hey!" Joe said appreciatively.

Now I had no idea what was going on. "Joe, how does he . . . ," I began.

"Later," he said. "Just go with it."

One of Kijani's bodyguards cleared his throat. "Kijani, I know this guy. Ty and I go way back," he said. "If he says these kids can help, they can help." He glanced at us and shrugged. "Don't ask me how."

It took a little more convincing. But finally Kijani nodded.

"I will wait," she said. "But only a little while. At the first sign that girl's life is in true danger . . ."

"Got it." Joe smiled at her. "Don't worry, we're on the case."

Joe called Frank as we jogged toward the stage area. He spoke to him briefly, then hung up.

"They're on this side, about ten yards back from the stage," he reported. "They couldn't get any closer. The place is swarming with security, and nobody's allowed up on the stage."

I nodded. I was still kind of confused about what had happened with Tyreese and Kijani. But I was willing to go with it as Joe had advised.

We rounded the corner and came within view of the stage. Sure enough, bright green security T-shirts were everywhere. Most of the guards were lined up in front of the stage, keeping the spectators back. A few crouched on the very edge of the stage itself. But nobody was going close to the huge fabric screens set up to block the view of the back half of the stage. Those screens had been in use all day during set changes, but this time, they looked ominous. Was Deirdre back there with her captors? Or was only one of the assassins up there waiting for Kijani while the other held Deirdre in a secret location?

"So what's our plan, anyway?" I asked Joe.

"Got me." Joe shrugged. "Let's see what's up, and we'll play it by ear."

That didn't sound like much of a plan to me. But I wasn't exactly bursting with ideas at the moment myself. Maybe the Hardys were used to this sort of thing.

But that didn't mean I was willing to give up. "There they are," I cried, spotting Bess's bright blond head in the crowd.

Soon we were all together again. George and Bess both looked pale and anxious. Frank was frowning, a little crease forming between his eyebrows as he paced back and forth.

"Frank," Joe told him breathlessly. "You'll never guess what Kijani just told us. . . ."

He'd almost finished telling the others about Kijani, the Death Brothers, and the rest of it when feedback squealed out of the speakers again. I spun to look at the closest video screen, but it remained dark. A moment later, a voice came out of the speakers.

"We are still waiting," the voice said. It had a strong accent.

"That's him," I said. "One of them, I mean. The scar guys."

"Perhaps Kijani did not understand our previous communication," the voice continued. "We shall now provide her with a visual explanation."

Once again, I stared up at the video screen, waiting to see what they meant by that. It wasn't until I heard shrieks and cries of horror from all around the audience that I realized I was looking in the wrong place. Spinning around, I saw that someone had just hit the controls to pull the privacy screens back from the stage.

That's when I saw Deirdre up there.

"Oh man!" Frank breathed, while Joe let out a string of curse words.

Deirdre was standing on the little platform where bands usually put their drum sets. Her arms were stretched up over her head and tied together, held up by a cable hanging down from the rigging above.

"Are those *wires* attached to her arms?" Bess cried, squinting.

A second later, an oversized image of Deirdre appeared on the video screens. Now everyone could see the thick wires snaking out from both arms, both legs, and the top of her head.

"How'd they get her up there without anyone seeing

them?" George wondered. "And what's with the wires?"

Joe shook his head. "I'm thinking they're planning to end this concert with a real bang."

"Right." Frank looked grim. "If they don't get what they want, they'll electrocute her."

FRANK

CHAPTER 19

WIRED

I was horrified by the whole situation. How could we have let it get this far?

The least I could do was make sure no more innocent bystanders put themselves in danger.

"Listen to me," I told Nancy, Bess, and George. "Joe and I can handle this from now on. You guys better sit tight and stay safe."

Nancy glared at me. "Not on your life," she said. "If it wasn't for us, you two wouldn't have figured out anything about this case until right now, along with everybody else."

"Hey," Joe protested. "That's not true!"

"Never mind," I told him. I stuck one hand into my pocket, checking for the earplugs I'd brought along.

"While you two were gone, George and Bess and I were talking, and we may have a plan. See, George is pretty good with computers, and Bess and I figure we should be able to . . ." My eyes widened. "Hey! What are you doing?"

Nancy had just sprinted off toward the stage. "Guess she's not in the mood for more talking," Joe said. "I happen to agree. We're way beyond using Google for help here."

With that, he took off after Nancy. I gritted my teeth. So much for my nice, clean, logical plan. It was bad enough dealing with my brother, Mr. Impulsive. I hadn't taken Nancy for that type at all. Live and learn.

I had to go after them so they didn't get themselves in hot water. But first I grabbed George by the arm.

"Listen you guys," I told her, glancing at Bess to make sure she was paying attention too. "Think you can get things moving on our plan without my help?"

The both nodded. "We're on it," George said. "Don't worry."

I was already worried. Very worried. I could only hope they both knew what they were doing and could handle a little fast action under pressure. Normally I wasn't one to count on people I didn't know for something so critical. But what other choice did I have? So I just nodded and then took off after Joe and Nancy.

I'd just spotted them up ahead when I heard a gasp

go up from the crowd. The bad guys had finally stepped into view on the stage.

My jaw dropped. Other than the mismatched scars, the two men were identical. Okay, maybe one was an inch or two taller, and the other slightly broader across the shoulders. But it was no wonder they'd caused such confusion.

The Death Brothers.

One of them stepped forward. He was holding a microphone. Under the bright stage lights, the scar bisecting the right side of his head shone like a vein of silver against his dark skin.

The second man hung back in the wings, clutching an object about the size of a digital camera. I couldn't make out what it was.

"Good afternoon, music lovers." The first man's voice bounced across the crowd, amplified at top volume. "I see that the security detail is creeping closer. Do not try anything stupid. As you can see, my brother's finger is already on the controls."

The second guy held up his hand. One of the cameras zeroed in, and the big screens showed a toggle switch with multicolored wires coming out of it.

The power switch, I thought, glancing at the wired-up Deirdre.

Death Brother #2 waggled his finger. Deirdre let out a piercing scream.

"See what I mean?" The first man chuckled. "That was only a taste of what we have in store for this young lady. Unless Kijani arrives soon, her dear friend will soon have the full meal."

I put on another burst of speed. A moment later I reached Joe and Nancy, who were huddled at the foot of the stage, whispering to each other. Several security guards were nearby, but their gazes were trained on the stage. The thug was still talking, ordering them to back up.

"Hey," Joe greeted me, his eyes glittering with adrenaline. "We came up with a plan. Nancy's going to try to distract the bad guys. Then you and I can take them out!"

That didn't sound like much of a plan to me. I glanced up at the stage. Each Death Brother had to be close to four hundred pounds of sheer muscle. Joe and I didn't even weigh that much together.

Too bad Tyreese had confiscated our cattle-prod gadgets. They might have given us a fighting chance. Without them, I couldn't see how we had any chance at all.

"Hold on," I said. "Let's not do anything crazy. I was trying to tell you before, George and Bess and I came up with something I really think will—"

"Shh," Joe shushed me. "I think I see the cops coming. Hurry up!"

He gave Nancy a shove toward the stage. I lunged

forward, trying to grab her before things got really out of control.

But she was too quick for me. Within seconds, she had darted past the security guards and vaulted up onto the stage.

"Hey!" one of the guards cried. He started to climb up after her.

"Halt!" Death Brother #1 yelled. "Do not come closer, sir, or my brother will hit the switch again." The guard backed off, and the thug strode forward and grabbed Nancy by the arm. "You," he said. "Who are you?"

"I'm here to trade myself for Deirdre," Nancy said. The microphone was close enough to pick up her words and broadcast them to the entire concert grounds. "You can hold me hostage instead. Just let her go, and I won't fight you."

A sort of awed moan went up from the audience as they watched. Out of the corner of my eye, I saw a bunch of blue uniforms moving toward the stage from the gate. The police officers who had been investigating the LI incident must have called for backup.

The whole situation was looking bad. I had to do something before someone did something stupid. I followed Joe, who was sneaking along the front of the stage toward the wings.

"Joe," I whispered into his ear, "listen to me for a

second, okay? I'm telling you, I was talking to George about what's happening here, and she . . ."

Before I could finish, Death Brother #1 spoke again, drowning me out. "I have a better idea, young lady," he said, leaning closer and sort of leering into Nancy's face. "Perhaps Kijani will be more convinced if we simply keep both of you hostage! What do you think, brother?"

He turned to look at the second man. For the first time, Death Brother #2 cracked a smile. It was horrible. And not just because of his crooked, yellowish teeth.

"Let's go!" Joe shouted, leaping into action. He swung up onto the stage and rushed toward the pair.

I had no choice but to follow. Joe and I were a team, and I wasn't about to let him go in alone, no matter how lame-brained his plan might be. Besides, the two men looked startled and a little confused. Maybe this would work after all.

And if not . . .

I cast a quick glance out at the crowd, searching for any sign of Bess and George. If things got bad, we hadn't given them much time.

Joe flung himself at the guy with the switch, so I took on Mr. Microphone. The guy let out a loud "Oof!" as I barreled into him.

I'm pretty sure I let out an "Oof" too. Trying to tackle that guy was like running headlong into a cement wall.

He swayed, but stayed on his feet. His face was twisted into a mask of fury as he came at me.

"Run, Nancy!" I yelped, seeing Nancy standing there looking kind of stunned.

I ducked and weaved, barely dodging the blow from his heavy fist. Maybe if I went for his legs . . .

Before I could come at him again, I heard a click. Glancing over, I saw Switch Guy holding a deadly-looking pistol on Joe.

Click.

When I looked back at my guy, I found myself staring down the barrel of another pistol.

I froze and glanced at Joe. He shot me a helpless look back. Nancy was just staring at the thugs, looking scared.

Trust me, I knew exactly how she felt. If Bess and George didn't come through . . .

"Fine." Mr. Microphone sounded a little breathless but still confident. "If two hostages are better than one, four must be better yet."

NANCY

CHAPTER 20

OVERPOWERED

I was horrified by this turn of events. *So much for that plan,* I thought.

I'd known all along that the thugs probably wouldn't go for the hostage-switch thing. But I'd hoped if I could keep them talking, it might give the Hardys enough time to figure out what to do.

Unfortunately the Death Brothers weren't feeling very chatty.

Soon the thugs were marching the three of us toward Deirdre. The first guy had stuck his microphone into his back pocket so he could hold his gun with one hand and shove Frank and me along with the other. His brother was still holding that electrical switch in his free hand. He used the muzzle of his gun to prod Joe along.

"Can't you see this is a lost cause?" Frank spoke up, glancing at the thugs over his shoulder. "You'll never get away with it. There's no way you can get yourself and Kijani out of this concert, let alone out of the country."

"Don't be so sure," the first brother said. "It is amazing what one can accomplish with a couple of hostages at hand."

I gasped. A *couple* of hostages? *They're not going to let all of us go even if Kijani does turn herself over to them,* I thought. For the first time, I felt an uneasy shiver of real panic. These guys were totally ruthless, and they were playing for the highest of stakes.

"If you turn yourself in, you might just get deported," Frank went on. "Or at least get reduced charges."

"Yeah," Joe muttered. "Dream on, Frank."

As we got closer, Deirdre did her best to twist around and look at us. "Nancy?" she called out weakly. "What's going on here? I demand answers!" She let out a sob. "When my father hears about this . . ."

"Shut up, you silly American fool," Death Brother #2 snapped. I realized it was the first time I'd heard him speak. His voice was raspier and deeper than his brother's.

"Is that any way to talk to a lady?" Joe joked.

In response, Death Brother #2 gave him a hard shove with his gun, sending him stumbling forward. Death Brother #1 chuckled.

"I believe what my brother is saying," he said, "is that he'll talk to her any way he pleases."

I stared up at Deirdre. The wires attached to her arms and head swayed in the slight breeze, making them look like multicolored snakes.

Snakes with the deadliest of bites.

Just then the speakers let out a sudden sharp whine, making me jump. But my gaze never left Deirdre.

There had to be a way out of this situation, if only I could figure it out. . . .

"All right, kids," the first thug said. "Stand in a line, please, so I can tie you up. Do not try anything stupid—my brother will be watching. And he is an excellent shot."

"Look," Joe said, backing up a few steps as the man came toward him. "You really don't want to do this. You've got to admit, it's not the best plan."

"He's right," I said. "There are thousands of witnesses out there, not to mention all the TV cameras. If you harm any of us, there will be no escape for you anywhere in the world."

Deirdre let out another sob. "Let me go!" she wailed. Her words were almost lost in another brief crackle of feedback from the speakers, this one even louder than the last.

I glanced at Frank, wondering why he wasn't saying anything. I was just in time to see him pull something out of his pocket. Then he reached up toward his ears.

I blinked, confused. Were those . . . earplugs?

At that moment, my entire head exploded. At least it felt that way. The speakers had suddenly burst to life again, and if I'd thought the sound coming out of them was loud before, it was nothing compared to this. The noise hit me like a physical blow, filling my brain and leaving no strength to breathe or react in any way.

Falling to my knees, I pressed my hands over my ears. I think I was screaming with pain, but it was hard to tell. There was no way to hear anything but the eruption of sound coming out of the speakers.

I was vaguely aware that the two thugs were also on their knees. I squinted over at them, trying to figure out if they were causing this somehow. The gun dangled from the first brother's hand, while the second brother had dropped both gun and electric switch on the ground, and was clutching his head and howling with pain.

Joe was writhing on the ground beside me, and out of the corner of my eye I could see Deirdre's mouth stretched wide in a scream. I could only imagine how the audience out front was reacting.

And then there was Frank. His face was twisted in a grimace of pain, but unlike the rest of us, he was still on his feet. With two or three swift steps, he reached the fallen gun and kicked it off into the wings. Then he stepped over and grabbed the first thug's pistol as well, tossing it well out of reach. The guy was too weakened by the wall of sound to resist at all.

The . . . earplugs! I thought as I stared at Frank. *But . . . how did he . . .*

The aural assault stopped as suddenly as it had started. For a moment, I thought I'd simply gone deaf. My head felt as if it were expanding like a balloon, ready to float away into the sky.

I shook my head, trying to gather my wits. Cries from the audience and moans from the others started to penetrate my shocked eardrums. As I glanced around, trying to figure out what had just happened, I saw Death Brother #2 roll over and stretch out his hand toward the fallen electric switch.

"Look out!" I yelled, my own voice sounding weirdly muffled inside my own head.

Joe saw what was happening and dove toward the man. But he was too late. The thug grabbed the switch and held it up.

"Time to teach you a lesson," he snarled.

He threw the switch.

I gasped, not wanting to look over at Deirdre. But there was no way I couldn't look.

Nothing happened.

Deirdre closed her eyes and cringed, clearly expecting the worst. But a second later, she opened her eyes again.

I gaped at her, confused and still a bit woozy from

the noise attack. A second later a stampede of police officers and security guards reached us, and I stepped aside to let them by.

"Frank," Joe gasped, watching as several officers tackled each thug to the ground and a couple more started untying Deirdre. "What just happened?"

Frank reached up and removed his earplugs. "What was that, bro?" he asked. "I couldn't hear you. These things are great—no wonder Dad recommended this brand."

"Huh?" Joe blinked.

Frank grinned at him. "Nice backup plan, huh? I spent, like, *hours* thinking it up."

"Are you sure you're okay?" Ned asked me for about the fifteenth time.

"I'm fine." I patted his hand. "Just speak up a little, okay? It's going to take a while to get my hearing back."

Ned nodded. "You and me both. I'm just glad I was still backstage in the tent when it all went down. All we had was a little auxiliary video screen, and some-body kicked out the plug a few seconds after the speakers went crazy." He glanced around at the others and shrugged. "Of course, that means I still don't quite understand what happened out there."

He wasn't the only one. An hour or so had passed since the Death Brothers had been taken into custody, but I'd spent most of that time giving statements to the police and getting checked over by medics. We'd all just met up again and found an open spot on the grass with a good view of the stage. The concert crowd had thinned out a bit, but the people who were left had mostly gone back to eating, drinking, dancing to the background music on the video screens, and playing Frisbee. Even after all that had happened, the Royal We insisted they were still going to perform, and it seemed quite a few people were willing to wait.

Frank hung up his cell phone and glanced up. "Okay, our report is in," he told Joe.

"Did you tell them about . . . um, you know." Joe glanced at Ned, Bess, George, and me.

"Not exactly." Frank made a face. "I said we'd had some help, and just let them assume it was from other ATAC agents."

Joe laughed. "What they don't know won't hurt them."

Frank looked a little uncomfortable. "Don't be too sure," he said. "They said they *might* send another team, remember? What if they didn't? They'll know we blew our cover."

I wasn't particularly interested in any of that. "Okay, I've already figured out that you guys were behind what happened." I glanced around at Frank, Bess, and George. "But I still have one question. How?"

"Two words," Frank said. "Backup plan."

He glanced at his brother and sort of smirked. Joe rolled his eyes.

"Whatever, dude," he said. "You're brilliant. You're superhuman, okay? Now lay off."

Bess giggled. "Quit teasing him, Frank," she said. "You said yourself you never would've thought up that plan if you hadn't put your hand in your pocket and remembered those earplugs."

"Earplugs?" Ned looked perplexed. "Why did you have earplugs in your pocket?"

Frank cleared his throat, looking sheepish. "Well . . ."

"Don't ask, man," Joe said with a laugh. "He said he was going to plug his ears for Lethal Injection's set, but I thought he was kidding. I didn't think he'd actually *do* it!"

"A lot of people suffer hearing loss from loud music." Frank frowned. "There've been studies . . ."

"Whatever, grandpa!" Joe laughed again. "So anyway, I get the earplug thing. But how'd you manage the rest? You were right up there onstage with us the whole time."

"I kept trying to tell you, but you wouldn't listen," Frank said. "The girls and I came up with a plan while we were waiting for you to get back."

"You mean *I* came up with the plan," George said. "I was the one who said it was too bad we couldn't drop one of those big speakers right on those guys' heads."

Bess giggled and brushed a piece of grass off her pant leg. "Yes, but Frank was the one who thought up the *actual* plan."

Frank smiled at her. "Thanks. But without you two, it never would have happened. Not only was I off chasing my crazy brother"—he paused to shoot Joe a look—"but it would've taken me forever to figure out how to hack that kind of complicated, state-of-the-art sound system. I still can't believe you two were able to do it in time!"

"Believe it," I said. "If anyone can hack into a computerized system in record time, it's George." I shook my head. "But I still don't understand—how'd you guys get access to the system in the first place?"

"It was easy. Those thugs had locked up all the techs in a closet somewhere so they couldn't interfere," George said. "So there was nobody around to stop me from just walking over to the main board and doing whatever I wanted with the sound system."

"Right," Bess added. "*After* I picked the lock to get you into the control room backstage."

I smiled as Joe turned and goggled at both of them.

"Let me get this straight," he said. "You two purposely deafened everyone by cranking up the speakers, *and* disabled the electric wires so those guys couldn't fry Deirdre after all?"

"Yeah, go figure," George said. "Who ever would've thought I'd actually lift a finger to save *her* of all people? But anyway, I only fixed the speakers. The electrical system was all Bess. She's great with that stuff—she's saved me from electrocuting myself lots of times, right, Nancy?"

"Right," I said.

Joe still looked stunned. Meanwhile I was nodding, satisfied to have all the pieces fall into place. I'd always known that my two best friends were talented, not to mention good under pressure. But I knew they couldn't have put together a complicated plan like that so quickly on their own. Frank must have had a lot to do with that, even though he was being pretty modest about it and sharing the credit. I had to admit it, I was impressed.

And not just because of the final plan. At first I'd thought the Hardys were mostly bluff and bravado, like way too many guys I'd met were. But the more I got to know them, the more that first impression was fading away. Sure, Joe might be a little impulsive. But he was also brave and funny and intense and really dedicated to helping people. And Frank, who had seemed overly conservative at first, had turned out to have an amazingly cool, quick, and creative mind under pressure.

No wonder they're in ATAC, I thought. *They must do stuff like this all the time. It must be so satisfying knowing they're making such a real difference in the world. Maybe I should talk to them about it a little more, find out exactly what's involved . . .*

Before I could figure out how to start, a roar went up from the crowd. I glanced forward. The Royal We had just run out onto the stage.

Kijani stepped up to the microphone. "Welcome, Rockapazooma," she said in her musical accent. "Sorry we are late. I'm sure you all know by now that the delay was due to enemies of the environment doing their best to turn back the hand of progress in my part of the world. That's exactly why these sorts of events are so important for raising awareness among caring people everywhere. The band and I wish to thank you for taking part today, and for your wonderful patience. We will do our best to make it worth the wait."

Cheers rang out from all around. Up front, people rushed to get closer to the stage. But I was happy just sitting there, and watching from our nice little grassy spot.

As Kijani continued her introduction, I noticed that George was frowning. "How annoying is it that Kijani was actually going to sacrifice herself for Deirdre Shannon, of all people?" She grimaced. "Guess DeeDee was telling the truth about them being best buds."

I hesitated, trying to figure out how to tell her the truth without setting her off on an anti-Deirdre rampage. "Well . . ."

Joe beat me to it. "She's not friends with her," he said. "Kijani had no clue who Deirdre was."

"Really?" George eyes lit up. "Awesome!"

Ned looked amused. "Oh right, I meant to tell you," he said. "I heard Deirdre talking to the TV people backstage, and I think I solved that little mystery. It seems she went to some high-dollar environmental fund-raiser with her parents last month. That's how she got the tickets to this concert, and it's also how she met Kijani and a few of the other performers . . . in the receiving line before dinner."

George let out a sharp bark of laughter. "No way!" she said. "Oh man, am I going to have fun with this. . . ."

Just then, the Royal We's drummer rapped out a fast beat, and the band launched into their latest top forty hit. The crowd cheered, many people getting up to dance along.

"Whoa, I love this song!" Joe jumped to his feet in front of us. Then he glanced down with a sheepish smile. "Oops, sorry. I'll get behind you so I can boogie without getting in your way."

Frank climbed to his feet. "Me too," he said. At Joe's surprised look, he grinned. "Hey, you're not the only one who can appreciate a hot tune, you know."

I smirked at his use of "hot tune." Not too cool, but funny.

As they bopped around to stand behind us, Bess

leaned closer to George and me so she could talk without bothering the Hardys, Ned, or other nearby spectators. "Take it easy on Deirdre, okay, George?" Bess put a hand on her cousin's arm. "She's been through a lot today. She doesn't need you giving her a hard time on top of that."

"Whatever. I'm not *totally* heartless." George grinned. "I'll give it at least, oh, two or three days before I start harassing her."

Some things would never change. I rolled my eyes and glanced over to see if the Hardy boys had overheard her.

"Hey," I blurted out. "Where did Frank and Joe go?"

Ned glanced over his shoulder. "I don't know. They were just here a second ago."

I stood up and looked around, but there was no sign of the pair.

"Uh-oh," George said. "Looks like they gave us the slip again."

I frowned, annoyed—and grudgingly impressed. Talk about a quick escape!

For a second I thought about going after them. It had only been a few seconds, and they couldn't have gone far. And everyone knows I'm pretty good at finding people, even ones who don't want to be caught.

But as the Royal We finished their first song and immediately started another, I let out a sigh and sat down again. Maybe it was better just to let them go.

I stared at the stage. When Ned reached over to put his arm around me, I relaxed back against him. But I couldn't resist one last glance around for the Hardy boys.

I'll let them get away with it this time, I thought, humming along with the music. *But they'd better look out if our paths ever cross again. . . .*